Lonar and the Gem of C'Vard

Anders Clark

For Dad, my first and biggest fan

THE FIERY BREATH OF HIS OPPONENT singes the hair on his arm. Lonar knows he will have to move fast if he is going to avoid the inevitable blow that is to follow. The one weakness a dragon possesses is its predictable attack sequence. Lonar sees the tail of the red dragon coming his way and with what little might he has left, he musters a jump, in the nick of time. He feels the rush of smoke-filled air pass through him as his feet again touch the ground. He is quick to steady himself and take up a proper fighting stance. He has been taught the essentials of dragon slaying since he was a young boy. To his left, he can hear a deep thud as his brother's shield is skimmed by the front claw of the green dragon. Lonar knows that if he turns his head to check on his brother it could be a fatal mistake. Instead, Lonar glares straight on as the red dragon drops from the sky directly in front of him, kicking up so much dust that the enormous creature is hidden. Before the dirt settles, Lonar is running directly at the dragon, his anger quashes any fear a normal person would being experiencing.

Lonar and his family have been warding off dragon attacks for as far back as stories have been told. Since he was a child, dragon assaults have been a regular part of his routine. The primary variation being the size of the invading force. It is determined by how brutal the last battle was, but for the most part, it is three at a time. Lately, the attacks have been getting more frequent and increasingly devastating. Something has the dragons as single-minded as ever to annihilate the entire Gragin clan. Lonar is never concerned with why; his job is to fight, to defend his village, his family and the kingdom of Zulbarg. It is a ridiculous dance whose music never stops.

Lonar throws down his shield as he approaches his current nemesis and grabs his other small blade from its snug position on his left calf. He tugs it free with one pull, not missing a step. Both of his weapons are in place, his left hand is level with his chin and his right hand drops back closer to his waist, ready to plunge forward with all of his strength. The dragon, too, is getting into a striking pose. It drops its head toward the ground so as to be able to get a full on inferno aimed at his challenger. Lonar knows what is coming but is certain that he is fast enough to prevent his own demise. As the dragon begins to take a deep breath in, Lonar reaches his target and forces his right hand forward driving his sharp blade deep into the side of the dragon's face. The force is enough to make the dragon lose his breath and give Lonar time to pull his blade from its flesh. The dragon lifts his head in anguish, before Lonar is able to free the sword, tossing him into the air. This also releases his stuck weapon. Lonar feels the air beneath him and can tell from the sight of the rooftops that he is far too high to hope to land safely.

Lonar drops his head and chest down forcing himself into a backward somersault until he is facing his foe. As his body reaches its apex, Lonar knows he has to act or the dragon will feast on his broken body the minute it hits the ground. He pulls both of his arms back as far as he can, then, one at a time, he flings them forward releasing each sword with great precision. His first shot is dead on; the dragon is disoriented by the blade sticking into his eye. The pain is so overwhelming that the dragon flops to the ground on its side, shaking the entire village. The second shot piles into the felled dragon's forehead. It stops moving. After seeing this, Lonar has time to consider his fate.

He closes his eyes and waits for the end; satisfied with his kill. Without having much time to contemplate it, the force of the ground is coming fast. Then, he bounces back into the air. He does not know much about anything other than fighting but he knows that is not supposed to happen. He begins to drop back down, more slowly this time; he feels the pressure on his back again but notices that once more it has some give. He laughs, realizing he has fallen onto an awning of one of the village shops. This time when he lands the awning splits wide open dropping him to the ground. Lonar does a mental inventory to make certain everything is still in working order. He is content that it is. Recalling that he has no shield and no sword and his people are still fighting for their lives; he looks around for anything he can use to replace his lost weapons. Off to the right, a glint of the sun catches his eye. He knows what it is. He takes a glance at the two remaining dragons and charts the best path to get to what he is certain is going to be his saving grace.

Lonar kneels behind a large barrel. A dragon's tail slides by as it goes off in pursuit of another villager. As soon as the dragon passes him; Lonar sprints across the town never taking his eye off of the shining beacon. Lonar reaches down, the knuckles of his left hand dragging through the dirt; he grasps the long wooden handle of the spear lying on ground near the blacksmith's area. He rolls onto his back, tossing the spear across the front of his body. Like a magnet, the spear attaches itself to his right hand as he leaps to his feet. Turning toward the dragon that had just passed and stretching out his left arm to aim, he hunches forward and balances himself with his feet planted in the ground. In one swift expulsion of energy the spear shatters the air around it as it embeds itself into the back of the dragon's skull. Lonar watches in approval as his second kill of the day drifts downward to its final resting place.

As the dragon's body hits the ground the village roars. Its chin hits a cart causing its neck to snap back. Lonar's skin twinges as this new position makes it look as though the dragon is staring right back at him. Lonar cannot help but sense that something is strange about the sight. The dragon's face appears sad, as if it knows it is dying and more than that; it cares. Screams from behind him bring Lonar back to reality. He turns toward to the fighting in the field, to see that the last dragon is retreating into the forest of Hugret. It steals away with a variety of armaments sticking out of bleeding wounds. The few remaining vanquishers cheer in victory. Lonar surveys the many broken bodies on the ground. His heart sinks recognizing one of them as his elder brother.

Two

LARSYNTH SHIVERS AT A COLD WIND blowing through her soul on the still and hot afternoon. She pulls her arms to her chest, giving herself a hug. Her long chestnut hair spills around her face and shoulders as she hunches forward. She braces herself for the soon to follow putrid scent; she knows she will never get used to that part. She wrinkles her nose as it hits her. No one around notices her odd behavior considering the immense heat of the day. As soon as the uncomfortable prelude passes, Larsynth straightens up and prepares for the main event. She looks about the scene, calculating where and how it is going to happen. A bolt of excitement shoots through her; she loves being here for this. Most NecroSights believe that they are meant to be witnesses of death and not to interfere with the natural order. Others, like Larsynth's father, believe that this is their gift and it is meant to be used. Larsynth is not yet sure how she feels about it, as a moral issue, but she loves the challenge. She saves as many people as she is able to but as a game; not because it is her given duty to preserve anyone's life. She thrives on the excitement and sense of power it gives her to cheat death of the prize it seeks. She continues to look around trying to figure out how she is going to outsmart her invisible foe this time. She sees it; the slow-motion, fast-forward of some poor soul's last minutes alive. While everyone else sees an old woman hobbling through the busy marketplace, Larsynth sees the haze of the attacker behind her plunging a dirk into her back and the unsuspecting crone falling lifelessly to the ground. From a NecroSight's point of view though, it is a mass of black smoke which forms itself into the characters and plays out the scene before dissipating back into the air.

Larsynth recalls the first time she ever witnessed such a frightening sight. She had been traveling with her father for as far back as she can remember and has no other family. NecroSights never stay in one place for long or allow others to become too familiar with them for fear of being discovered. So, they lead a nomadic life which suits her fine as she bores easily and is always ready for the next adventure. Her father had decided that it was best not to tell his young, friendly daughter of her family's heritage. He feared she would either inadvertently tell someone about their secret or the idea of it would scare her as it did him when he was first told about the gift at a much too young age. Larsynth was eight years old when, walking through a marketplace similar to this one, she felt the cold chill and smelled the horrid death scent. She could not figure out what was going on and began to cower behind her father's robes. He pulled her up into his arms and held her tight whispering in her ear,

"Everything's going to be alright, Smidgen. Don't be afraid. I've got you."

He tried to protect her from seeing, fearing she was too young. But her eyes caught sight of the black smoke parading about imitating an old woman grabbing her chest and falling to the ground. Larsynth thought, at first, that the pantomime was funny, a joke of some kind. She could see right past the smoke and watch the same old lady wandering about just fine, shopping without a care in the world. The smoke dissipated and then she saw the woman grab at her chest, her eyes bulged out as she gasped for breath before falling to the ground. Larsynth yelped in shock and horror. Her father, who still had a tight grip on her, pushed her head into his chest as he turned, leaving the marketplace looking for a secluded spot to explain what had happened to his frightened little girl.

"Are you scared, Smidgen?"

"A little," she put on a brave front so he would be proud of her.

"It's time to tell you something important. But it's a big secret. You must promise to never tell anyone," Dervile looked his daughter in the eyes so she could see how serious he was about this.

"Promise." Larsynth kissed the palm of her right hand then reached it out to put it on her dad's heart.

He did the same.

He told her about their people and their gift and that it was his belief that whenever possible they should try to help these poor souls avoid the hand of death but that sometimes, as with this old lady, it was beyond their abilities. Larsynth understood all that he said as best as possible for a small child. Now as she has grown she considers her ability more as a great power than a gift and tends to treat it as such. She is always willing to play the game. As it is, one has now begun.

Larsynth takes off. She pushes her way through the crowd and grabs a large platter from a dealer's table and lifts it up behind the old woman as if to admire either the intricate carvings, or her own reflection, a bit closer. As she raises the plate a sharp ring lets out and the assailant shrieks in pain. She smiles to herself as she bends over to snatch up the weapon. She turns to the man and asks if his hand is alright. He glares at her, his eyes searching her face for some sort of explanation as to what happened. His disbelief and pain overtake him. He is not able to comprehend how she has pilfered his dirk or that the old woman has now disappeared in to the crowd unaware of her reprieve. She wants to laugh at his stunned silence but instead decides to get on with her shopping. She slips the dirk into her pocket and continues her way through the bazaar looking for anything of interest. She cannot help but look back over her shoulder at the man still staring at the hand he is now cradling. He looks up at her in time to see her smirk. She flicks her flowing chocolate hair back over her shoulder as she strides on in victory.

Three

"**L**ONAR, SON OF HULZER, ARE YOU READY for The Retelling?" his uncle announces.

It is the time in the Feast of Soul's that Lonar is dreading. While he respects the customs of his people, to him, this is pointless. The last clash with the dragons was devastating. Five have survived; himself, his younger brother, two cousins and an uncle. They are all gathered at the sacred Mount of the Feast to celebrate those who have died in battle and to ask them to hold a place for them in Metalor. He cannot help but to feel a bit silly retelling the story to only four others who, he knows, have heard it at least a dozen times in the last quarter cycle. Any one of them can recite it in their sleep by this time. He is not sure if this privilege is supposed to bring comfort or merely a distraction but he accepts the need to follow tradition. He knows his brother would have wanted him to do so. The thought of pleasing his older sibling brings him a pang of sadness that tears through his whole body. But it is, after all, the curse of the Gragin clan to have to pay for the misdeeds of their ancestor, Sharsin, until the last of the dragons has either been destroyed or has departed from this land. Lonar knows all too well the story of Sharsin and the dragon. But tonight, for the first time, he contemplates the tale of how his people became destined to be the dragon slayers of Zulbarg as he retells it to the few Gragin survivors.

"This is the first story of our people. I tell it to you as it was told to me. Listen carefully, as you will tell it to those who will come after I have been struck down gloriously in battle, as my father before me," he fights back his emotions at the mention of his father who he lost in a raid two cycles ago.

"We celebrate his honor as we celebrate the honor of all those who died beside him in our great calling." The words spring forth.

"To Metalor!" The other four declare, not merely the fate of their loved ones but a fate they, themselves, know is close at hand.

Lonar closes his eyes recalling the first time he was permitted to participate in the Feast. His brother pointed out every important detail of the ceremony, explaining anything Lonar did not understand. He remembers the deafening roar as the men made this statement, in those days there were closer to 100 of them at the Feast to celebrate their fellow clansmen; in sharp contrast to the meager five left today.

"How pathetic we must look to them from their place in Metalor." Lonar thinks to himself. He is determined to give his brother's well-earned commemoration the honor and dignity it deserves. He pulls back his shoulders and continues louder than before.

"Shortly after the beginning of time, Sharsin, the first mother of Gragin, walked through the forest of Hugret gathering bark and berries. She came upon a cave far to the west." He points toward it.

"She entered the cave, as she had every right to do." He makes certain to articulate that point, as is custom.

"She got lost in the cave and desperately searched for the way out when she saw a brilliant light. She knew this was her way back home so she followed it. But when she got to the source of the light she found a room piled high with stacks of gold and gems. This was the most incredible sight she had ever seen. Gold surrounded her. But, she was an honorable woman and knew that surely this all must belong to someone. So, she decided to carefully leave and not touch anything. As she turned to go, she came face to face with a horrible creature, a dragon,"

The men hiss at the word.

"She had not seen anything like it before. This creature snatched her up and squeezed her tight in its gruesome claw shouting at her that she would die."

Lonar makes a sideways fist to illustrate the dragon squeezing the unfortunate woman.

"Sharsin was terrified and begged for forgiveness. After ten days of torture the dragon agreed to let her go. But only if she swore to him that she would never tell another soul where his cave was hidden. She agreed and ran back home. For three years, Sharsin kept her promise to the ferocious dragon. Until one day, a traveling merchant came to town. This man had seen dragons and knew of the great treasures they kept hidden away. He believed that someone from the village had to have known where the dragon lived so he put a magic charm over all the people while they slept."

He makes a sweeping motion with his arm. He has seen this played out by so many others he has all the movements memorized and knows when to use them to emphasize the important parts of the story.

"The next morning, without control of herself, Sharsin told the merchant what she knew. Off the merchant man went to find the treasure. The same dragon who caught Sharsin also captured the man. The merchant told the dragon that Sharsin did not keep her promise and that the whole town knew about the treasure and was planning a raid on the dragon. Being an honorable person he could not stand for such treachery so he came himself to warn the dragon of the attack."

Lonar's face shows the disgust all Gragin still have for any traveling merchants.

"The next sunrise, a dozen dragons attacked her village. A handful of Gragin survived."

Lonar looks into each of his remaining kinsmen's eyes and can see that this part of the story weighs on them too.

"But they flourished in spite of the new enemy. Though Sharsin never intentionally betrayed the dragon, we Gragin have kept the kingdom of Zulbarg safe from the loathsome creatures for centuries. It is our destiny to protect Zulbarg, and so we fight as our ancestors did and we will continue to fight!" Lonar raises his fist high into the air, the other men follow.

"To Metalor!" Lonar calls.

"To Metalor!" His kin answer.

Lonar throws himself back into his seat beside his uncle.

"You did your brother great honor with that Retelling, Lonar." He clasps his hands on Lonar's shoulders.

"Thank you, uncle."

Lonar is relieved that it is over. He is spent. Important decisions will have to be made the next morning and Lonar is in need of sleep.

Four

LARSYNTH STRUTS THROUGH the marketplace flitting from table to table handling anything she thinks might be of interest. At one dealer's stall, she finds a small silver gilded hand mirror. She sizes up the merchant pondering whether or not it is possible that he is more round than he is tall. She shakes the thought from her head noticing how he waddles rather than walks and that his arms are too short so that he cannot fold them in front of himself. He appears cheerful and kind; she knows he will be an easy target.

"Sir, can you please tell me how much is this adorable mirror? My granny will love it," she asks in her cutest and most charming little voice. The merchant has not yet turned his attention away from his current business dealing.

"I'll have to take a look at it closer," he grumbles from the other table finishing that transaction.

He shuffles over to the mirror. Looking, for the first time, directly into her face his features soften. She is a natural beauty. Her elegant hair matches the deep chocolate brown of her eyes which she has learned how to use to her advantage when dealing with most men. Her attire is not out of the ordinary for a young female of Dabrilas who spends most of her days traveling. Her leather pants closely mimic the chestnut color of her hair and eyes, as do her knee high boots. Her dress is cinched in at the waist with a matching brown leather belt that is four inches wide. Drawing a line straight up from the middle of her belt are five cream buttons that correspond with the scalloping trim of her forest green dress. Her bow and the quiver on her back are clues as to her wandering way of life. The two long slits of her dress running up each thigh as well as the open front of her skirts below her belt indicate that she lives a life that requires easy mobility.

"What a sweet girl you are to think of your granny. For you, 5 pieces." The merchant replies.

Larsynth gives her best pout as she flicks her long eyelashes. Her looks give her a definite benefit but are not so overwhelming that she causes a scene. Most people do not notice her walking by but are often struck by her attractiveness only after something draws their attention to her face.

"Oh no! I don't have that much."

She sulks pretending to put the mirror down; certain to make a good show. She speaks loud enough so that the kindly looking older gentleman beside her can hear the scene as well. She always says it is better to try to catch two fish, in case one gets away.

"I was really hoping to make this birthday the best ever before she moves away." Larsynth wipes a fake tear from her eye.

She cannot contain her smile as both the merchant and the man beside her frown in sorrow for her predicament. She figures if she does this just right she may be able to get the mirror from the merchant and some flowers from the stranger. A large hand comes in from behind her and snatches the mirror out of her grasp. Before she can react in a manner that will be appropriate for her current character she hears the familiar voice;

"Don't worry my dear, I have already gotten a gift for granny."

Larsynth grins at the shop keeper as relief wipes the empathy from his face.

"Come now, we don't want to be late for granny," her father growls tugging her away from the table.

Larsynth feels the dirt and hard gravel grinding on the tops of her toes as her arm is going to be pulled from its socket. Her father has a tight grip on her wrist and is not about to let go.

"Daddy, stop! I can walk myself. Let go of me!" She begs.

"Larsynth!" his thundering voice shakes deep in her chest. "You will not act in such a deceitful manner. We are not liars or beggars"

She is ashamed, not for what she has done but because her dad, of all people, caught her. She cares for little in this world other than herself and her father. His opinion of her means everything and she can see that she has hurt him.

"We may not have a lot but what we do have we got honestly."

She knows that he is not angry merely because she is being deceitful but also because he is embarrassed. She has made him feel insufficient and she knows she will never forgive herself for that.

"I don't really want it. I just wanted to see if I can talk him down on the price." She defends.

"Do you think I don't know what games you play? The way you get weak willed men to buy you things? You will get a reputation and that will risk exposing us. Are you willing to have that happen?" He asks not wanting an answer.

"Daddy, that won't happen. You're over reacting." She insists.

She fears that he is about to tell her that she is not allowed to go back to the market.

"Oh, you think so? You don't know what it was like before and you should be glad." He warns.

She knows this is not the time to point out that NecroSights have not been slaves for a thousand years and that he had not been alive then either. But she knows that his parents told him of the horrors and it is as though he had lived through it himself. Nothing scares NecroSights so much as a return to those awful days.

He lets go of her wrist and takes a step back away from her in disgust. She studies her dad trying to read how severely she has messed up this time. He is a giant to her but always a gentle one. His silver hair dusts the tops of his shoulders whenever he shakes his head at her, usually out of amusement in spite of himself. But that is not the case this time; he is not amused. She longs to see the wrinkles on his forehead and beside his eyes appear like they do anytime she is able to make him smile or better, to laugh. She adores her father more than anything in the world and hates herself for all the pain and frustration she knows she causes him. He bends down and softly takes her by the shoulders,

"No matter how many millennia I live I will never stop protecting you from the terror that I know will befall us if anyone ever discovered who or what we are." He softens his voice.

She knows that he is right. She can see in his eyes that this fear haunts him day and night and she again feels the sting of disappointing him.

"I promise, no more. I'll do better at staying hidden."

She kisses her palm then stretches it out to his chest.

"Not this time."

He lets go of her and smiles. It is clear that he wants to believe her. She knows she has to change the subject and a small reminder of the good things she does will not hurt.

"I saved a woman at the market today." She boasts.

She tries putting her arm back at her side. As the words leave her mouth she wonders how he will react. She knows that he will be pleased that she saved someone but will the risk of being caught set him off again?

"I was really careful, no one noticed a thing." She adds reassuring him.

"Some thief was going to stab an old woman in the back but I blocked his dirk with a plate. It was actually funny. He couldn't figure out what happened." She continues.

Larsynth pulls the small blade from her pocket and hands it to her father, like a trophy. She can see his eyes relax as he looks in his hands at the gift. She beams.

"Excellent work, Smidgen." He cheers.

It is clear that he is as relieved to move on to something else as she is. He turns the dirk over in his hands before giving it back to her. Something about it is odd to him but he cannot figure out what. He pushes aside what he is sure it is just his annoyance with his daughter.

"Time to head back." Dervile declares.

As he stands up, Larsynth notices that even when he is doubled over like that her father is still taller than she is. It is times like these when she stares in awed admiration of him. He gathers up their belongings and starts to pack their bags.

18

"Going to get dark soon. You ready?" His voice breaks the silence.

"Yep, let's go." She agrees, situating her quiver as she reaches for her bow.

Five

LONAR KICKS A PIECE OF CHARRED wood still lying in the village center. Most of the small shacks are unrecognizable by now. He marvels at how easily his people had been able to rebuild and get back to life as normal every time an attack interrupted a day's events. Now that nearly everyone is gone, all that remains is rubble. He loves them for their resilience but today he is not able to recall that pride for their fortitude. Instead, he is awestruck over the unprecedented number of casualties from the last battle. The remaining five Gragin gather together at the town well. For a long time, no one speaks. Their sadness hangs thick in the air along with the ashes of their once lively home. The men's chests tighten as they can sense the ghosts of their families, friends and ancestors milling around them. The apparitions are waiting to hear what the survivors plan to do next and how they will honor those who have gone before them.

"I guess it's time to work."

Lonar's uncle declares with a sigh. He bends down to pick up a singed piece of wood but stops when he realizes the others are staring in his direction.

Lonar's younger and last remaining brother, Laithor, declares, "I believe that it is time for the last of the Gragin to leave this accursed place."

Laithor's eyes fill with tears as he exhales releasing the last bit of hope he has. Lonar surveys the destruction also concluding that his home will never likely see its glory again.

"Uncle Deycin, I will follow your lead in all things but I believe we should consider what Laithor has said," Lonar's cousin, Croscet, steps forward dropping his gaze in disgrace.

Deycin looks at each of them in disbelief, "in spite of this overwhelming defeat it is the solemn duty of the Gragin to defend the people of Zulbarg." He glances toward the castle, "The people of Zulbarg are innocent bystanders who are made to suffer for the crimes of the Gragin. It would be dishonorable to leave the people on their own against the dragons. Especially since they have never fought them before. They would be slaughtered. I'll not have their blood on my hands."

Deycin vows with determination reproaching the others for even considering such a shameful act as giving up and leaving.

"A lot of good the five are us will do to defend them."

Croscet throws up his arms in anger. Lonar can see where both of them are coming from but he struggles to decide who is right; his concentration breaks as his brother moans.

"Neither option is sound. Of course, Uncle Deycin is right; we can't abandon our ancestral obligations. But so is Croscet, the most that the five of us can do at this point is buy the kingdom another few days. Those awful creatures know we're all but wiped out," he growls as he narrows his eyes in the direction of their lair. "They'll be back and I doubt they'll wait long."

"Then we fight until they finish the job, if they can." Deycin boasts without much cause.

"Is it our duty to defend Zulbarg or merely to die at the hands of the dragons?" Croscet challenges his uncle.

"Then what?" Lonar asks. "What is the third option?"

All of the men stand silent before Deycin's son, Dransis offers,

"The five of us can't stay. It'll be akin to suicide and we won't really be helping the kingdom. One more raid by those evil devils and we'll be wiped out and the path to the people is clear for their annihilation too. We have to teach the King's army the ways of fighting the dragons before the last of us is gone. That way the people aren't left defenseless."

Lonar muses, "'before the last of us is gone'"?

He looks around at the dejected faces of the remainder of his family. His eyes scan their sore, bleeding and broken bodies. Lonar believes deep in his bones that all is lost, his people have failed.

"What if it's too late and the only thing this accomplishes is to get a greater number of people killed? If the dragons are capable of wiping out the entire Gragin clan what chance will some unprepared soldiers have even with their training? How much time will we have to train them?" Lonar begins to doubt that there is any solution at all.

Deycin adds, "The attacks have been coming so frequently I doubt the King's army will stand any more of a chance against the creatures than we have, after all, we're born to fight the dragon scourge. It has always been the Gragin's responsibility to keep the dragons as far away from the people as possible; which is why the Gragin never lived inside the city walls but built our own small village to the west; to keep the dragons from attacking the castle."

"Won't the dragons see that the soldiers are being sent out from the walled city and decide to directly attack it?" Croscet wonders.

Dransis spells it out in a way the others know is true but do not want to admit.

"No matter what new plan we consider it may well end up a disaster for the people of the kingdom and the Gragin will have failed."

Deycin looks to Lonar, "Either way, we must send someone to go see the King and ask at least for reinforcements for now. It must be you."

Lonar is relieved at the thought that the King will be a wise man with many advisers and that they will be able to come up with a more reasonable idea. He is emotionally exhausted and is not sure how clearly he is thinking. He decides that it is time to push it all aside and leave it for the brighter men that he will find at the castle. Now, for the second time in his life, Lonar is going to travel to the walled city.

As he reaches the edge of the village he surveys his journey ahead. The castle is down in the valley below where his clan had set up their community all those years ago. It will take less than half a day's walk to see the King. He knows that if he is swift he can meet with him yet today, rest there for the night and be back home by the afternoon meal tomorrow. Lonar decides to make haste and be on his way. Not expecting this journey to be too out of the ordinary, Lonar could never have imagined how this trip will turn his world upside down so quickly.

Six

LONAR REACHES THE CITY GATE well before
evening meal and is confident that he is on schedule.
He has little doubt that the King will be eager to
speak to him. Throughout the history of Zulbarg the Gragin have
always been honored guests of the King anytime they found
reason to visit.

"I am Lonar of the Gragin clan to the west, protectors of
Zulbarg from the evil dragons. I must see the King. It is of grave
importance." Lonar declares to the watchman.

"Yes, of course." He replies.

The guard snaps alive as he shouts to the others to open the
gate and escort this man to the King. Lonar bows his head in
recognition of the sentry's understanding of the importance of
being hurried. The massive door sounds like thunder as it shows
the way into the protected city.

"Come with me," another guard directs.

He has seen a couple of Gragin in his life but the image of
them never ceases to both amaze and chill him. He tries not to
stare. This man in front of him is the epitome of a Gragin warrior.
His long hair, rather than each strand flowing together with the
others, is made up of what looks like a nest of thick snakes all
charmed to do his bidding. The color of his skin matches his hair,
matches his armor, and matches his boots; all of which are the
light brown color of a tree trunk. Which is not a bad description
for the build of the man himself. He has never seen a Gragin's

arms covered by sleeves and he is certain that is because there either is not enough material or time to bother doing so. Instead, they wear a boiled leather tie-down vest with small metal studs running throughout, along with plain leather pants. The only color to be found when surveying this incredible image are the clear green of his eyes. Which are now beginning to narrow at the sentinel, bringing him back to the task at hand.

The guard walks the impressive Gragin through the bustling town. Lonar was a small child the other time he had been here, yet he feels the same wonder now as he did then. There are more people in this little area than he has ever seen in one place. There must be close to a thousand people here. The largest the Gragin ranks has ever swelled to had been 400, but that was long before his time. Lonar tries to keep an official air about him as this is a vital mission but his senses are overwhelmed. He is impressed by the soothing hum of the town. Everything is moving like a well-choreographed dance. The merchants in the market sing out to the shoppers, the best of them attracting the most people to their table. His mouth waters as they pass a shop with fresh baked bread.

"Best bread in all the land," the man barks out to him noting Lonar's interest.

The guard scowls as they continue on through town. Lonar does his best to keep pace with him as he pushes his way by the crowds. They come upon the blacksmith, Lonar is comforted by the familiar clang of the hammer. Every Gragin male is trained from a young age to forge his own weapons and this craft is something Lonar enjoys. He loves the satisfaction of creating something rather than destroying it. There is a flash of pain as an unruly spark singes his arm. He is accustomed to the burning and finds it reassuring. It is nice to be in a place full of life, unlike his tiny village, which is now a graveyard. He is saddened at the thought of his home and his people. He has been so caught up in the excitement of this strange place he has nearly forgotten the destruction of all he has loved; the guilt cuts deep.

Breaking his concentration, Lonar feels that something has a hold of the back of his tunic. He turns in time to see a tall gangly man with flowing white hair look him directly in the eye and say,

"Eclant. I am Eclant."

The man looks crazy; he is sopping wet, hunching his chest and shoulders to the left while ringing out his hair with both hands. Even wet, his white hair is strikingly bright compared to his dingy cream colored robes. Lonar looks down at the man's feet noticing a small puddle forming but does not see any type of trail to indicate from which direction the man has just come. He scans back up to the gentleman's face but instead sees the tips of his hair flying upward as the rest of his body hits the ground. A child had run by, knocking him over. The youth glances back and giggles as the unfortunate elder struggles to his feet. Lonar tries to suppress his amusement at this strange man as he reaches out a hand to help him up. Lonar decides he is harmless and smiles as Eclant thanks him.

"Watch out for the little ones," Lonar warns as he turns back to the guard to continue on his way to the King.

"Crazy old fool," the guard spits at Eclant, "pay him no mind. We're almost there."

Lonar is anxious to meet with the King but is now excited to investigate the town further after he has finished his business.

As they walk into the castle and pass a few more guards, Lonar is struck by the difference of the atmosphere inside the castle as to outside in the city. The castle interior is cold and dank. Everything is gray stone. As far as the eye can see, the floor, the walls and the ceiling are all stone. It gives Lonar an eerie feeling. He ignores it as he prepares what he is going to say when he meets with the King.

"Wait here." The guard commands more forcefully than he had yet spoken to Lonar.

He stands outside the chamber entrance trying to retain a tight grip on his nerves. He thinks about his father, he thinks about the dragons he has killed, he thinks about his people and the story of Sharsin as he relives the previous night. He knows that it is up to him to make the King aware of their failing but he is determined to do so with honor. He will not hide his people's defeat and refuses to make any excuse for it. He will make the King aware, offer himself for any necessary punishment and return home with reinforcements.

"Come," the guard says as he peers out of the curtained opening.

Lonar's legs feel heavy as he takes his first steps into the presence of the King. He stops, breathing in deeply and reminding himself that this is his duty. With renewed courage, Lonar storms into the chamber and without so much as a glance around the room he declares,

"My King, I am Lonar, son of Hulzer of the Gragin clan. I have come with unfortunate news. There are only five of us that remain. We are strong and will continue to fight until it is our time to enter Metalor but I fear the kingdom is not safe."

"Is this so?" the King interrupts.

He pushes himself up from his seat at the long wooden table with what looks like maps sprawled all around it and stares into Lonar's face.

"How does it come to pass that the great Gragin clan has fallen?"

Lonar cringes at the remark, recognizing the King's sarcasm when he spoke.

"The dragons, Majesty, they have been attacking with a frequency never before seen. We are unable to keep them at bay. We have failed our King Cryptis and the entire kingdom of Zulbarg. I have come to accept punishment and to secure more soldiers and women so that we may continue to fight and to repopulate our ranks."

Lonar is careful not to look the King in the eyes. At first, he is impressed with how unalarmed the King is but before long is baffled by his bizarre responses.

"You shall have no punishment other than the pain of your loss. I won't care to waste my time. You may take whatever women go willingly. They are of no consequence to me. But soldier's you may not have. I care little of the Gragin and never have. Go back to your village and tell the others the King no longer requires your service; as it is insufficient anyway." The King mocks.

Lonar knows that he should not contradict the Ruler's wishes but without soldier's, they will all die. There will be no point in returning with any women. Not having any new soldiers to back them up will mean their deaths anyway. None of this makes any sense to Lonar. The Gragin were always held in high regard by the previous Kings.

He studies King Cryptis as he tries to process what is happening. He can tell that without his royal cloak he would not be an impressive man. He is scrawny with black stringy hair. His face is pale and his eyes are a cold, black void. This man looks more like a rodent than a King. Lonar feels an urge to strike him but knows far better than to act in such a treasonous way. He gathers himself and swallows his anger.

"But, your Majesty, without more men the few of us remaining will not be able to protect the castle from attack. The dragons have become more blood thirsty than ever. I fear for the people of your kingdom."

Lonar cannot believe that he should have to explain this to the King. Surely, he understands.

"Do you take me for a fool, man? Am I not King? I say no more men! If the dragons will come, let them come. I have no fear of such things. Now leave."

The King throws himself into his seat and returns his attention to his maps. Lonar stands in silent disbelief before the guard that escorted him there takes him by the arm. Lonar yanks it free and marches out of the chamber in anger and confusion. Once again the warrior has failed.

Lonar wanders around town enjoying the night air and trying to clear his head. His encounter with King Cryptis has him at a loss. This is not at all how he expected his visit to turn out. What is he to do? Is it time for his people to move on? If the King no longer wants them there then they should go. But they are Gragin; that is all they know how to be. What will they do now?

He cannot believe how silent the city is at night. How crisp the air is. He is in a daze considering what his future may hold; for it is clear that everything is changing. He wonders how his brother and uncle are going to take the news. Will they blame him? Is there anything he could have said differently? Could he have pushed more to make the King see? He is sure there is no more he could have done. The King is not concerned about the dragons. Lonar cannot get beyond that thought in his head. How can he not be worried about them? Does he not care about his people at all? Even if he doesn't care for his people he has to realize that if the dragons attack the city they will surely kill him too. Lonar's head spins around and around like this as he meanders about town in a stupor. The moon catches his eye and pulls him out of his trance. As he stares at it, he decides that it is time to rest before his trip home. He heads back to the inn where he had secured accommodations for the night earlier in the evening.

Lonar feels some unseen force knock him to the ground. The next thing he knows he is on his stomach with someone on top of him.

"Oh, my word that is dreadfully precise now isn't it? I do apologize. That must have been an extraordinary show of concentration on my part won't you say?" The oddly familiar voice remarks in the dark.

The boney man is attempting in vain to remove himself, but all the flailing about is only managing to make matters worse. The third time his hand comes toward Lonar's head he grabs it and grumbles,

"Stop and let me."

"Yes, a much better plan I'd say."

The old man stops moving as Lonar rolls on his side clearing the floundering wretch off of his back. Lonar springs to his feet then looks at the wreck on the ground still lying immobile. Lonar rolls his eyes.

"I meant for you to hold still a minute not for the rest of eternity."

He grabs the man by the waist and stands him up, recognizing Eclant by his actions more than his looks.

"I suppose that was silly of me. I do not really have degrees of motion it's usually all or nothing with me, you know."

"As a matter of fact, I don't know." Lonar does not want to be annoyed with the man but cannot help himself.

"Yes, right, of course, you won't." Eclant clambers on incoherently.

"So, you okay then?" Lonar asks hoping to end this latest peculiar encounter.

"Yes, fine, sure." Eclant starts. As he notices Lonar walking away he panics, "No, no I'm not. I'm... broken. My left ankle."

He says picking up his right leg.

Lonar narrows his eyes and chuckles,

"Well, you seem to be standing on it fine."

Eclant changes legs before exhaling with exhaustion from the useless charade.

"No, you see, what I mean is I have important information for you. It's about the King and the dragons. You see..." Eclant's voice trails off as he looks right passed Lonar, "Oh no, not already. Yes, of course, well there was me landing on you and the falling and all that... I guess it did take some time but really..."

In a blink, he is gone. The odd character vanishes right in front of Lonar. He cannot believe what he has seen. Is this some type of magic? He stands there staring at the spot Eclant had once occupied before he decides it must be his mind playing tricks on him. He tries to shake his head clear. He fears that everything he has known his whole life will change the next day and resigns himself to a night's sleep.

Seven

LARSYNTH EXHALES AS SHE LEANS BACK against the trunk of the large tree. She adjusts her position as a bit of bark scratches her. She is drained from the long journey and more than a bit frustrated by the fact that her father refused to let her out of his sight all day. He even went hunting with her for the midday meal. He coughed so loud as she was about to release her bow string that it made her miss the critter at which she was aiming. It heard the whizzing of her arrow and took off. Her usual 30-minute hunting venture ended up taking two hours. She knew there would be some repercussions from her previous performance at the last town but is annoyed by his constant supervision.

Her father is out gathering wood for a fire and she was instructed to set up for the evening. But she wants to revel in the silence and explore her own thoughts before preparing the meal. She breathes out and closes her eyes. She feels the movement of the ground beneath her feet. She reaches back and grabs a hold of the tree trunk for support. As the it becomes overwhelming she gets the sensation that she is falling. She her stomach is dropping and her heart is floating jarring her.

Larsynth's eyes open as her whole body jerks in anticipation of hitting the ground. She presses her hand so hard into the tree now that she winces in pain. She looks around, surprised to still be standing, she chuckles at herself and releases her vice like grip from the bark. Pulling her arms in front of her, she presents her right palm to her face to inspect what damage she has done. A small chunk of bark protrudes from it which she plucks from its spot, tossing it to the ground. She scans around in hopes that her father has not returned and witnessed the whole embarrassing episode. Larsynth begins clearing the ground to provide a proper location for the evening's camp. She has become so focused on her task that she does not noticed her father's return.

"What happened to your hand?" He asks.

Her father frowns at her, seeing that she is protecting it. His eyes show their disapproval at her carelessness. She looks down at the small hole in her palm.

"Oh nothing, I scraped it on the tree. Find enough wood for the fire?" She changes the subject.

She knows there is no possible way that she can explain what happened without her father thinking she has lost her senses. Another day of him hovering over her is unbearable.

"Sufficient, yes."

He eyes her then turns back to the small game beginning to dress it for their meal.

"Insulvar is a beautiful little town, I think you will like it. There are a lot of young people for you to meet."

Larsynth rolls her eyes knowing all about the town of Insulvar. It is well known throughout Dabrilas as the most honest and honorable of places. The people are legend to be descendants King Postin's time. As the story goes, nearly 500 cycles earlier there lived a King named, Postin Probar. King Postin is said to have been determined to bring about a new code of living. He believed that through trust only can love actually live and that love itself is the single true virtue of life. Therefore, he set out to create a community of pure love. It is still a place of honor, truth, humility and hospitality. People from all around Dabrilas often speak highly of their visits to Insulvar so that in turn more people desire to visit. Traders will often forgo other, more lucrative, towns and cities in order to peddle in Insulvar. They know they can sell their goods with little haggling, no fear of theft and a great amount of hospitality and happiness. Insulvar has become the center of the trading world even though its location is out of the way from many of the larger kingdoms. Among the more cynical, Larsynth included, there is the belief that the King's hidden motive for his utopia was in fact more trade. Which would provide more taxes with which he could live in luxury. Motives aside, his push for a moral society took a strong hold in the area. So powerfully in fact, that to this day being told that a stranger hails from Insulvar is a guarantee that he can be trusted without another word needing to be spoken.

Larsynth is aware of what her father is implying in his reference to the young people of Insulvar. She shrinks into herself out of shame. She is saddened by the realization that he thinks so little of her now. She knows that her deeds in the market have upset him but has not, until now, determined to what a degree that is true.

"Yes, I am highly thrilled at the prospect of making some friends when we arrive. I have always had a great respect for King Postin and his kin."

Larsynth hopes her comment does not sound to him as fake as it does to herself. She is desperate to please her father.

"As do I," he smiles to himself.

He knows his daughter better than to believe her admiration is truly as strong as she is pretending but he also knows that her comment is not meant as snide but instead is her honest attempt to gratify him. His heart melts for her. He has a desire to release her from the emotional punishment he has been imposing.

"Of course, they can be a bit of a dull group and somewhat pretentious in their humility. Wouldn't you say, Smidgen?"

He winks at her. She stands silent as the meaning of his words sink in. Her glee replaces the tense air as she falls into her father's arms for a grateful embrace. They both laugh. She knows her sins have been forgiven. She is overjoyed as relief fills her.

Larsynth returns her attention to the fire which she has been stoking with a renewed happiness. Her father hums as he continues to prepare the meal. She catches herself staring at one fixed point directly on the other side of the fire. She is certain there is something out there watching her. But she can see no evidence of it. Numerous times she tries to ignore the thought but it nags at her all through mealtime. Her father announces that it is time to rest as the next day will see them to another long journey. Larsynth stops preparing for the evening's sleep and is certain she hears something. She refrains from overreacting. She becomes convinced that whatever it is has been there for some time and is stalking them. She feels like prey; the anxiety is making her shaky. She is exceptionally perceptive, especially tonight. Larsynth walks around to the other side of the fire and peers out over the vast, flat and empty plain.

"Whatever are you doing, my child? It's time for rest. There is nothing out there."

Her father is confused by her behavior.

"Dad, I..." Larsynth comes closer so that she can whisper, "I think there is something out there, watching us."

"Impossible," her father replies not trying at all to keep his voice from being heard.

He pulls the thin blanket up over his shoulders and plumps his pile of clothes that will be his pillow. He is now annoyed at her obvious stalling antics. He is accustomed to her attempts to avoid going to sleep. As his head finds a satisfying resting position a new voice is introduced into to the conversation.

"I apologize if I made you uneasy." says the figure stepping forward out of the shadows.

She is startled by the sight in front of her. A man is standing in the exact spot that Larsynth has been surveying at all night. She cannot understand how she had not seen him earlier. An individual, a little taller than she, dressed in all black walks forward into the light of the fire. He wears a long black hooded cloak over his black leather pants, boots and a full leather shirt with long sleeves and a high collar. She is not prepared for what she sees when he pulls back his hood. His face is delicate and white like that of snow. By contrast, his hair is as black as a starless midnight and flows long down his back like strands of silk. His eyes are the brightest, clearest and most vibrant blue she has ever seen. Swinging from his hips are two elongated sheaths reaching to his knees. She tries to keep an eye on his hands to make sure he is not reaching for them but she is too busy struggling to keep her gaze focused on any one part of him as they drink in this haunting yet beautiful sight.

"I am Slagradislaun of the Franegler people." His voice is calm and steady.

He can see that they are startled by his presence but he is used to that reaction. Larsynth's trance breaks and she jumps to grab for a weapon as her father springs to his feet.

"Oh my fawn feathers! Who are you?"

He demands reaching for Larsynth. He is attempting to pull her away from the stranger in protection. All the while, she is wriggling away from his grasp. Larsynth is trying to keep her father behind her, also hoping to protect the one she loves.

"I mean you no harm," Slagradislaun declares raising his hands, palms out, to show that he is not holding a weapon. "I am not a thief or an assassin. I am nothing like the others. I am a traveler."

"A traveling Franeglian? I have never heard of such thing." The old man doubts.

"I assure you. I am no enemy of yours, Dervile the NecroSight."

Slagradislaun pushes a few strands of his long black hair out of his face. Larsynth is chilled to her bones at the sound of not only her father's name but at this stranger knowing it and knowing that they are NecroSights. Her mind races over the evening's conversation wondering if he had overheard them. Her recollection is void of any mention of who they are or of their abilities. How can he know all of this? She looks into his eyes hoping to find an answer there but it as though she has plunged into a cold pond. She is taken aback by how bright and clear his blue eyes are. They jump out at her in contrast to the deep, richness of his milky skin.

"I am Dervile, the simple trader," he emphasizes. "How does my name become known to you, Franeglian?" Dervile demands.

"You are a well-known *trader* in these parts." Slagradislaun is willing to play along.

"Please leave us, sir. There is no need for your presence and you succeed only in angering me." Larsynth declares.

She is shaken by the whole incident. She cannot imagine how this person has come to know their secret, nor the danger he can bring to them. Her primary concern at this point is to distance herself and her father from the stranger.

"I, myself, am but a traveler who is seeking the safety of others. I mean you no harm and I can promise you that your identities are safe with me. I wish to journey with you to Insulvar."

Slagradislaun continues in his laid-back manner to convince them that they are safe with him. Dervile cannot help but wonder at the absurdity of the thought that a Franeglian would need any aid at all. He knows of the people and they are superior fighters. Their movements are fluid and quick; they can scramble up a tree in seconds like a beast. He cannot believe that this stranger can possibly need protection of any kind; especially not from an old man and his daughter. Yet, something about him is safe and honorable. He is a slender creature, as are all Franeglian. Dervile towers over every one of the few Franeglian he has ever met in person. Their bodies are slim and fit and their reflexes are legendary. As a child, he had heard stories that the Frandeglian are so fast that one can smack you across the face without you ever seeing his hand move. Their temperament is also such that it is not unlike one of them to do just that. Of course, he would be smacking you as a distraction from his stealing your purse. Dervile is well acquainted with Slagradislaun's people but cannot stop thinking that this one is different from the others. His eyes are more peaceful and his nerves are more still. Dervile has no doubt that Slagradislaun could put down a Slither cat in seconds but trusts that he will not harm them. No, he is not to be feared. He senses that there is more to this stranger than meets the eye and is determined to get to the bottom of it.

"Sit."

Dervile commands pointing across from himself, near the fire. Larsynth's eyes bore holes into her father's skull as she tries to telepathically impress upon him that this is a bad idea. The old man has gone crazy, she is convinced.

"Yes, sir, thank you."

Slagradislaun is relieved that what he believed was going to be the hardest part of his mission is starting to work itself out; gain their trust. He lowers himself into the seated position and again pushes aside the few strands of hair that are constantly falling over the left side of his face. Larsynth stares at her father and then turns her gaze to him with intense examination he attempts to sound well at ease as Dervile drills him about his intentions. He can tell this is not going to be easy.

Eight

THE NEXT MORNING LONAR SETS OFF for home to pass along the King's words to his kin. He knows that a lot of hard choices are going to have to be made about the future of the clan. His journey back takes longer and is more difficult than the one to town. Not only is he emotionally sapped and preoccupied but the trail is uphill and the sun is hot on his back. He ponders the events from the day before; the bustling town with all the sights, sounds and smells overloading his senses, the horrid King, who clearly does not care about either the Gragin nor his own people, and the crazy old man appearing and disappearing out of nowhere. As he considers all that has happened to him, he fears his uncle will think that either he has gone mad or that this is all a joke or trick; these things certainly cannot be real. The King would never abandon the Gragin and a man appearing and disappearing by magic? It cannot be. Magic is in the fairy tales told to small children. It all has to have been in his imagination.

"Stress, I was under a great deal of stress after talking with the King. I never actually saw the man appear." Lonar recounts the events trying to talk it through so that it will make some sort of sense.

"The first time I saw him he was standing behind me, I have no idea why he was dripping wet in the middle of the town like that but, who knows?" He shrugs it off. "The second time, when he landed on me... He must have jumped down from the tower above; that has to be it."

Lonar has small relief as he continues to convince himself that the incidents with the strange man do make perfectly logical sense after all. He pretends, too, that the man did not disappear right in front of him.

"I must have looked away or had gotten caught up in my own thoughts and didn't notice him go into the shadows."

Now that is all tied up neatly and put aside in his head, Lonar decides it may be best to leave out the parts with the crazy white haired man altogether. It is more important to deal with the new issues brought on by the lack of cooperation from King Cryptis.

As he climbs the last precipice, his stomach rumbles. He still has more than an hour to go and while he is eager to return to his home he figures that a quick break and some berries may be a fine distraction. He sits down on a rock near a berry bush. Lonar pulls off one berry at a time and pops them into his mouth. This brief respite makes him realize how tired he is. He takes a deep breath arching his back and stretching out his arms to his sides. He blinks a few times and yawns. As he pulls his arms back to himself preparing to reach for more of his delicious snack he sees that his hands have become stained red from the fruit. He knows the image all too well as he has been a warrior all of his life but, for some reason, looking at his hands now with the berry juice as a reminder, his stomach tightens. For a wonderful but fleeting flash, sitting there on that rock, with the sweet smell of the berry bush he manages to forget. He forgets all of the pain, the sorrow, the despair and hopelessness. He forgets his family. He resolves that it is time to move on as he tries in vain to get the stains off his hands. He recalls a small creek up ahead and decides to proceed that way with an overwhelming need to clean off the crimson juice. Reaching the edge of the water he kneels down next to it and picks up a smooth stone, rubbing it over his hands attempting to rid them of the stain. A wind wafts in carrying with it the smell of something burnt. It is familiar to him as it fills his nostrils. His stomach drops. He bounds to his feet and runs toward home. His mind fills with panic. He knows the dragons are back. He knows that his four kin are all alone in the village holding off the attack, waiting for Lonar and the army sent by the King. He also knows that they will be fighting bravely. Worst of all, he knows that relief is not coming. Only he will come to their aid. No army will be marching in with him in triumph to relieve these weary warriors in battle. He will stand beside them, fight with them and die with them. He knows that this is going to be the end of the Gragin clan. His pace speeds beyond anything he would have thought he was capable of as he races to fight by the sides of his beloved comrades. His chest and eyes burn. He dances his way up through the trail; hopping over a fallen tree trunk, weaving around thorny bushes and ducking to avoid low hanging branches. His reflexes are beyond compare. He spots the landmark his eyes have been craving, the tiny hill right outside the village. Running through the clearing to the summit he sees it: everything is gone. He is too late. The battle is over. The rest of his family is dead. They are all gone. Smoke billows from the ruins carrying with it the soul of his once lively home. Through the gloom are the tails of two dragons flying back to their lair. His head drops in despair, the red stains on his hands are all he can see through his grief.

Lonar stands in the center of what little is left of his town. The fires rage on all around him. All that remains of his home are embers and ash. He is stunned by the scene, the only thing more gruesome than the toppled buildings are the remains of the last of his kin, slaughtered. For the first time in the history of the Gragin, there will be no Feast of Soul's after this battle. As he examines the remnants, his heart sinks; the realization that he is now the last of his kind takes ahold of him. He walks toward the corpses of his fallen relatives, the black smoke chokes him and burns his eyes making them water in defense. A few steps away from the ravaged body of his uncle, Lonar spies several strange disturbances in the ground where it has been dug up. Something about this scene gnaws at him. The destruction is far too vast and unnecessary for what it would have taken the dragons to finish off so few men. He cannot imagine how this type of thing would occur during a battle or even as the dragons finished tearing apart the village. He looks around the ruins of the town seeing more of these peculiarities. He considers the reasons behind these strange sights and grows enraged. Lonar contemplates possible explanations concluding that it was a finishing blow. The dragons came to not only massacre his few remaining brethren. They also set out to demolish their little city, his home. These acts are savage and dishonorable. His head turns from one sight of destruction to another; he becomes dizzy and increasingly irate. The hatred the dragons have for the Gragin propelled them to not only kill everyone in Lonar's village but to make sure to lay complete waste to the town as well, to wipe away any proof of the existence of the Gragin at all.

There is no other reason for the dragons to have done this. It is the worst possible insult. This is an attempt to erase any memory or evidence that the Gragin has ever existed.

"Then, they will succeed," he declares.

Lonar picks up the largest log he can find. He grabs it with both hands and stands it up on its end. He can rest his chin on it. He wraps his hands around it in the middle as if picking up a person by the waist. He hoists the giant log up and rests it on his right shoulder. He takes one final look around the battered and dying village. He trudges over to the nearest building staring at it. He pulls the log back over his right shoulder. He swings it, landing a hard blow to the corner support of the little burnt building. The last of the strength in the shack gives away and the small hut falls to the ground. Lonar watches, imagining his uncle's final fall to his death.

He goes from building to building bringing each one down with a blow from the log. As they fall in succession, he thinks of a person he has loved. The beams of the building become their arms and legs and the crumpled pile on the ground is their broken bodies. The last bit of smoke is their cries of pain and tears. The crashing sounds of the huts hitting the ground are their accusations and displeasure for Lonar. He bears witness to their massacre. He knows they are right to curse him; he has failed them. Once the last one is demolished, Lonar drops the log as he walks back to the little hill top to the east of the village, the spot where he first discovered that he is too late. He sits, looking at the final destruction of his home; at the bodies of his kin. The sun begins to set on him and his home, Lonar knows what he has to do. There is no future for him; he is the last of his kind. He will not roam the world bearing the shame of being the coward who did not die with his clan. He pulls himself to his feet and with one last look at his nightmare, he marches off into the forest of Hugret to find the dragons' cave.

Nine

LARSYNTH, DERVILE AND SLAGRADISLAUN are packing up camp for the long day's journey to Insulvar. Larsynth cannot keep her eyes off the new addition to the trip; she does not trust him. She can tell her father does but is not able to figure out why. Her father is not a trusting person so it is unusual for him to take a liking to someone new so quickly. She has faith in her father's instincts but she cannot get over Slagradislaun so openly admitting to knowing that they are NecroSights. He did not say it in a threatening way, she has to admit. Still, she is terrified that he may turn them in or sell them off as happened so often in the old days. That is the reason all NecroSights have to keep their secret hidden and now this complete stranger waltz's into their camp announcing he knows all about them, including her father's name. She cannot understand how her father is not leery of him.

"Lars, are you ready to head out?" Dervile calls to her.

"Yes, everything is prepared," she replies tying up the last bag.

"Excellent then, let us go." Dervile looks at Slagradislaun.

Larsynth keeps one eye on Slagradislaun at all times. She notes that he carries nothing in his hands. They are always empty. But he has a great deal on his back; a large pack, a rolled up blanket, and two canteens. Hanging from his hips are his two long daggers and she noted a glint of metal in the fire light coming from his shins last evening. It must have come from two smaller weapons strapped to his legs. His story of wanting to travel with them for his own protection is clearly a lie.

"Why are you going to Insulvar?" Larsynth askes Slagradislaun hoping to sound merely interested and not accusatory.

"It's a large trading city," he responds, offering no further explanation.

"It is," she acknowledges, "but why are *you* going there?" Larsynth does not want to sound snide but she can recognize a roundabout answer when she hears one.

"The normal reasons," he shrugs.

"Do you have anything to trade?" She continues.

"We'll see." Slagradislaun answers.

"Tell me about your people, Slagradislaun. I've never heard of the Franeglian before." Larsynth continues to press him for information.

"There's not much to tell," is his reply.

"Do you have any family?" she tries again.

"Yes, I am sure that I do." Is all he says.

Larsynth pulls back her neck at the odd response to such an inquiry. Dervile knows his daughter and does not doubt that she could continue like this all day. He also knows that Slagradislaun's people are not prone to over sharing or sharing any personal information at all for that matter. He wonders for how long he should let this exchange continue. For he, too, is curious about this stranger. Nothing about his character is reminiscent of a typical Franeglian. He smiles rather than sneers, his weapons are present but have not yet been brandished, he shows no interest in any valuables they may be carrying and makes no threats of any kind. What is more, is that he told these two unknown persons his name. Dervile has become aware of many Franeglian and has been in the company of a few but has never been told the name of a single one. This is the first time he has heard the name of a Franeglian. As a boy, there were rumors that they, in fact, do not name their offspring at all. Anonymity is so important that they do not bother with them. However, what is most astounding of all and is the primary reason that Dervile feels an odd sense of trust, is that Slagradislaun had slept, soundly, all night in their presence. He realizes that just because he has never been told a name of a single Franeglian in all his years it does not mean they do not have them, but he is sure that before now, no Franeglian has ever given in to sleep around strangers, not one, not ever.

"The Franeglian don't tend to stay together as families the way you are accustomed. They are a race of thieves and assassins because of a strange... quality they have. To be seen and yet unseen. It is known as the gift of OverSight," Dervile decides to break the silent tension.

"Like, they can be invisible?" Larsynth questions.

"Not really," Slagradislaun pipes in.

"No, they just have a strong tendency to be... overlooked." Dervile tries to clarify.

"But I'm looking right at him and can see him," She is confused.

"Yes, because you *know* he's here."

Slagradislaun has never had to explain to someone before what the Franeglian gift of OverSight is but he can tell this is not working and he does not like being talked about as if he is not standing right there. Especially when he *can* be seen.

"Remember last night before I spoke to you when you thought there was something in the woods?" He begins.

"Yes, and now I know that you were hiding out and watching us." Larsynth answers.

"Actually, no, I was standing right there in view the whole time. I was not hiding at all. You just couldn't see me." Slagradislaun explains.

"So, you were invisible?" Larsynth insists.

"More like unperceivable." Dervile inserts.

"Had you known I was there you would have seen me but since you weren't expecting me to be there your brain looked around me or over me."

"So, now that I've seen you you'll never be able to sneak up on me again?" Larsynth wants to be sure.

"Only if you expect me to be around."

"Well, I guess that would make being a thief or a killer much easier." She accuses.

Slagradislaun does not respond. He drops his head and watches the ground go by under his feet as they continue trotting on. Larsynth can tell that this has upset him. She knows that she should be sorry for her words but she cannot trust him yet. She studies his face thinking that she sees a tinge of shame.

"If he isn't like the others, why? How did he end up so much different from the rest? And how does he know us and what does he really want?" Larsynth focuses on all the questions she still has about Slagradislaun as they bombard her.

His people are not the only ones trying to be over looked. Her whole existence has been a struggle to keep others away from learning their secret. Her stomach drops again as she recalls that he does know who are and what they are.

"Dervile!" a shout breaks the silence.

All three travelers startle at the unexpected sound; each reaching for a means of defense as they turn around to face from where the voice came.

"Eclant, my old friend!" Dervile's face registers a great relief upon seeing the old man, "you look well."

Larsynth and Slagradislaun lower their weapons realizing that there is no danger here. The old men embrace looking like two tall majestic and strong oak trees getting their branches tangled together.

"As do you. Hello, Larsynth you look charmingly beautiful as ever." Eclant says turning her way.

"I'm sorry, sir," she says as politely as possible to her father's old friend, "but I don't recall the last time we may have seen each other so I'm at a loss for your name." She reaches out a hand to shake his as he takes her in a full hold.

His smile fades as he grabs her by the shoulders and pulls her away from him. Still with a tight grip he looks in her eyes and then to his surroundings. His confusion is apparent.

"I see Slag is here but what about the others? Where are they?"

"Slag?" asks Slagradislaun, "As in the crud that gets stuck on the bottom of your boots?"

"You're thinking of sludge, my dear boy," Eclant dismisses.

Slagradislaun looks around in utter confusion, his solace is the fact that Larsynth is as lost by this exchange as he is.

Turning to Dervile, Eclant exclaims, "This is all wrong! Are you even on your way to Zulbarg?"

"Zulbarg, why would we be going there?" Larsynth answers, confused by everything about this man.

How does he know her father and apparently her as well? Does he know their new traveling companion? Slagradislaun does not think so and is clearly put off by his little nickname, the thought of which makes her smile. She knows that will have to be the only way by which she will ever refer to him again.

"Why? Because of the dragons!"

As Slagradislaun hears the final word, his blood goes cold. "Dragons?" He exclaims.

Eclant continues on, not hearing. "Lonar and Neras need your help. Scratch that, the entire kingdom needs your help. That damned King."

He mumbles the last part under his breath before continuing. Looking at Slagradislaun, Eclant answers the look of confusion and concern on his face,

"I understand what you need from my friends, it's a wonderful and worthwhile cause and they'll help you I'm sure, but that is going to take some time you understand. They have to find out where the mirror is and then you'll all have to go get it...*that* will not be easy with all the... It's a whole thing. I hope you understand why we need to focus on this first. The dragons are dying off and none of it is their fault..." Eclant rambles.

"You must speak fast old man, if you slid here you haven't got much time to explain about Zulbarg---," Dervile starts but before he finishes Eclant is gone with a blink. "I hate it when he does that!"

"Dad, who was that? How does he know me?"

"I guess he's met you."

"I don't remember him"

"Oh, you may not have met him yet," Dervile answers, too distracted by what happened to explain.

Larsynth squints her eyes and tiltes her head to one side.

"So, how does he know *me*?" Asks Slagradislaun, "More importantly how did he *see* me?"

"Clearly, he knew you would be here with us." Dervile replies looking Slagradislaun square in the face. "The mirror? So, that's why you've sought us out? That's a tall order young man. Are you sure you want that? All of your people---?"

"Yes!" Slagradislaun replies before he can finish. "I know full well what it means but it has to be done."

Larsynth is annoyed at how cryptic the two of them are being.

"Mirror?" She asks.

"Dragons?" Dervile wonders.

"What's going on? Are we supposed to fight dragons or help them? Who was that and where did he go?" Slagradislaun questions.

"It sounds like he is concerned about the dragons dying off." Larsynth offers, mentally bouncing between the two topics.

"There has been an ongoing battle between the dragons of the mountains and a small clan outside the kingdom of Zulbarg for centuries." Dervile explains.

"So, he wants us to help the dragons against those people? Why?" Larsynth wonders aloud.

"I really can't imagine. I don't see how it can be any of our concern or his. I'm not sure what he thinks the three of us can do anyway." Dervile concludes.

"Well, you two do have a pretty handy gift when it comes to fighting." Slagradislaun adds. "And I'm pretty capable in that area myself." He says pulling out his daggers from their sheaths on his hips.

Larsynth rolls her eyes. "Our gift isn't for hire or used to fight someone else's war!"

Dervile can see Larsynth is upset by the mere suggestion and he can understand why. This is dangerous territory for NecroSights but he feels differently.

"My dear, I have known that man a long time and would trust him with my life and with my gift. I don't believe for one moment that his intentions are selfish or the least bit sinister. I'm certain that there is much more to it than we managed to get out of him in that short amount of time. But I do admit that the whole situation is odd and more than a bit confusing." Dervile says.

"I don't know, I'm not sure what to think. The whole thing is really weird. He knows me and Slag."

Slagradislaun shoots Larsynth an angered look at the sound of that name. She grins back.

"Where did he come from?" Larsynth demands.

"*When* did he come from is the real question." Dervile wonders.

Ten

THE FIRE SPRINGS HIGH to the top of the cave, crackling and hissing as its light flashes bright enough to illuminate the depths of the creatures' souls. The heat is welcomed and worshiped by the dragons. Their scales are alive. Their chants are loud and harmonious as they celebrate their victory and mourn those they lost. Yet, this time is different. An end is near and they all can feel the relief of it. They believe that the Gragin have been defeated, not a one yet lives. The ancient dragon tales told of the coming of such a day but after so many generations of fighting many have begun to doubt. Although the Gem is still not found, hope springs forth that the day is close at hand. And soon the dragons will return to their homeland of Narcor. The songs ring out. All rejoice and dance in the light of the fire. As the festivities wear down the dragons convene a meeting to determine the exact plan for the next day's hunt.

"The Gem must be hidden deep underground." One of the elders, Tralados, insists.

"No, no they are Gragins not dragons, they would not dig and bury their treasure. It's in a hut among the rubble." Kartort points out.

"No, it is in a sacred place. They wouldn't hide it somewhere as vulnerable as a hut." Aubamey adds her voice to the chorus.

The argument continues until it is decided that all ideas are valid. The search will include each possible location. The Gem of C'Vard must be found at all costs.

Neras listens to the conference with nothing to add. The excitement is overtaking him. He squirms, restless to begin the pursuit for the mystical Gem. The tragedy of the Gem of C'Vard has haunted his kin since it was stolen. Generations of dragon have sacrificed their lives in attempts to retrieve it from the evil Gragin and return it to its rightful place, with the dragons in Narcor. The account of how the Gem was pilfered from the proud dragons was first told to him when he was a young hatchling. He dreamed he might one day participate in the adventure of its glorious return.

Neras observes his brethren as they celebrate their time of triumph. They are proud but beaten. Their scars shine in the bright illumination of the fire. However, for the first time in many cycles, they look confident that the end of their suffering is near. Neras envies them. He was born undersized and strange colored and because of his deformities is not allowed to leave the cave. He is barely half the size of the dragons his age and is such a vivid cobalt blue that he is unable to blend in to the outside surroundings and thus makes an easy target. He has not been a part of the many years of warring with the Gragin and, in fact, has never seen one in person. But he knows all about them and their wicked ways. He is as familiar as any of them with the story of the Gem of C'Vard and the ancient task assigned to his people to keep it safe. He witnesses the sorrow and pain his fellow dragons must face every day since it was stolen out from under their protection. Each cold night is a stinging reminder of the consequences they suffer for their inadequacy.

"Neras, my friend, I have decided to go with you to the counsel for permission to join the search tomorrow." Kogad announces placing his scarred claw on Neras' left wing.

Neras struggles to straighten himself as the hardy force of his friend's gesture knocks him over.

"Thank you, friend. I am certain that my request will be approved. As the threat has now been annihilated there is no reason to fear for my safety."

Neras has waited for this day all of his sheltered life. When he was young and first able to realize that he is different he had a great amount of anger toward his people for shutting him away in such a cruel manner. He longed to fly in the warmth of the sunlight and fight alongside his kin to help secure their freedom from this cold, wretched cave. Unable to do so, he turned his attention to learning the ways of his people and to the art of listening and gathering information. He is always the first to offer aid to the returning fighters and has bandaged many wings and claws. He found comfort in the belief that he is helping the cause, if merely in his own small way. But now that will change. He is sure that he will be permitted to leave the cave with the others in the morning and help retrieve their Gem.

"Neras, the counsel is prepared to discuss your request. If you will come with me." The council master, Veralke, declares.

He is the oldest of the dragons. His scales are brittle and faded. Scars from the countless clashes with the Gragin pepper his form. The wariness of a life of a constant warrior show in his soulless black eyes. Tales say that he is the only one remaining who remembers life on Narcor. It is said that he actually passed through the portal to Dabrilas with the others. Neras is not sure if this is true, but it is possible. Whenever Neras questions Veralke about what life is like on Narcor his answers are short and he manages to find something else more important to do, leaving

Neras without much to go on. During the times when the rest are away fighting the Gragin, Neras likes to imagine what it would be like to return to the dragon home world, he envies Veralke's memories but also has compassion for the pain those memories must invoke.

A chill rushes up his spine and through his horns. He hopes his life is about to change. The small chamber where the council meets is cramped, for everyone but Neras. Being so small is a blessing and a curse. As the others in the cavern crouch and try in vain to avoid hitting their horns on the top, Neras stands comfortably without fear of bumping into anything, save a larger dragon trying to situate himself. His eyes search the faces of the council members trying to determine what they are thinking. The extraordinary events of the day make it impossible to tell. They are all exhausted but energized at the prospect of their torment being nearly over. One of the elders waves Neras into the center of the circle indicating that it is his time to present his case. He launches forward. Stopping, he remembers to slow down and hold himself with a bit more decorum. He stands up straight and lets his wings expand behind him knowing that this position makes him appear somewhat larger than he actually is. He had learned this trick early on. He gathers his thoughts and draws in a deep breath.

"Distinguished counsel," Neras begins, "I come to you today to beg that as my kin has so valiantly and honorably defeated the horrid Gragin scourge you will allow me, too, to do my part in freeing our people. I realize, of course, that my smallish size and bright hue have, until this point made me a possible hindrance to the cause, a fact which has brought me much sorrow over the years." He pauses for a breath.

"Yet, I do have a great desire to fight alongside my brave kin. I have willingly pushed aside my own yearning for the good of the entire group. Now that the threat has been vanquished, and I will no longer be a burden. I can be a great asset. I am small and will therefore be better capable of fitting into the petite dwellings of the Gragin to seek out the Gem. As having never before been to their town I may also have a fresh eye on possible locations that it may be hidden. I ask for the opportunity to participate in the great search that will bring our people the completed victory and our freedom to return home. Thank you"

Neras is silent. He looks at each member with hope. He cannot imagine any reason why they will not approve his request. At this point every bit of assistance is crucial. The members mumble amongst themselves for a time before turning back to Neras.

"You have been faithful and loyal to your people but we believe, though, that this is not the time for your first venture outside the cave. This search is of utmost importance and we believe that this new world may be overwhelming to you and cause us all delay. It is agreed that it will be better for your release from the cave to come after we have retrieved the Gem from the Gragin village. We know this is disappointing..." Veralke's voice trails off.

Neras lowers his eyes to the ground as the pain and rejection build up in his chest.

A new voice rings out from a small ledge above them.

"Gem? Is that the lie you all have spread through the generations? Is that the lie that has now destroyed my people and our home?"

The heads of the many dragons snap toward the sound. Neras, whose head had dropped in sadness a few minutes previously, now lifts it to see what this distraction is. His jaw drops as he sees standing on the ledge a creature he has never before witnessed. It is screaming and flailing around madly. A sword nearly the size of its body is in his hands swinging about violently. Neras has heard many stories of the Gragin people but never imagined that this is what one actually look like. He is struck by how *small* it is. He has always imagined the great foe to be well, greater. He struggles to understand what the creature is screaming about as his head takes him somewhere else entirely.

"This is it? This is the reason I have spent 92 cycles in this cave? This small thing is the reason I have never felt the heat of the sun or left my prison? It can't be." Neras thinks to himself.

Kogad, attempts to spread his wings to fly up to the ledge and snatch this nuisance and silence him forever but manages to fall sideways into Neras knocking him to the ground. His anger is growing and overtakes him. The same anger is filling the room, but for a different reason. The other dragons are fixated on this unexpected Gragin but Neras' rage is aimed at his own people. He lifts himself up off the ground and looks around the room, not at the dragons themselves but at their scars. He wonders how it can be that these tiny creatures have inflicted such damage on beings more the three times their size. They must be skilled fighters but it has to be more than that. Their cause has to be strong for them to defend themselves to such a degree. He looks from one battle wound to another and he hears the words the little man is preaching.

"My people have nothing of yours. There is no Gem hidden anywhere. I may be all that is left but I will defend

Zulbarg. I will not let you hurt those innocent people. Your anger is with the Gragin. Sharsin did give up your secret but only because the merchant tricked her. But nothing was ever removed from your treasures."

Neras thinks that this Gragin has gone insane.

"Certainly, being the last one left of his kind must have pushed him over the edge but what is he saying? He comes into the enemy lair knowing full well that he will die. Why would he be spouting off such nonsense?" Neras is overwhelmed by the sense that something is not right.

Being in the small cavern is in no way a hindrance to Neras, as it is to the others. They are scrambling around trying to figure out a way to get to the crazy Gragin but are unable to spread their wings. He spies a tiny ledge along the wall. He knows he is not too large for it. Neras rushes over to the side of the cavern avoiding the floundering wings of the larger dragons. He steps onto the ledge following it up toward the crazy shouting Gragin. He is going to show all of them that he is not worthless and how better suited he can be in some circumstance than the rest of them. The elders shout to him instructions to grab the Gragin and bring him back to them. They want to deal with the enemy themselves. Neras has the approval and usefulness he has desired from his kin for so long.

He reaches the landing next to Lonar. It is the first time in his life that Neras has stood next to another living thing that is actually smaller than him. He towers over the Gragin. The power is intoxicating. He realizes with how much ease he could end its life; a swing of the tail, a swipe of the claw or a small puff of fire and he will be the hero. He, Neras, will in fact be the one to finish off the last of the Gragin scourge. How sweet that would be. He has never felt so in control and yet out of control at the same time. He hears those below yelling commands to him. He turns to face his minuscule prey prepared to change his place in dragon history forever.

Eleven

"WHEN? WHAT DO YOU MEAN by that 'when is he from?'" Larsynth ponders.

"So, really who is that guy?" Slagradislaun chimes in.

"He is an odd character that's for sure but he's a good man and an old friend of mine and our people." Dervile answers with a smile looking to Larsynth.

"How does he disappear like that?" Larsynth questions.

"Under normal circumstance I would rather keep his secret safe as he has done for us for so long. Since he wasn't particularly cautious, I'm sure I can explain with a clear conscience. You see, Eclant is what is known as a Darist."

"A Darist? I've never heard of them," argued Slagradislaun.

"Oh, so it can't be true then?" Larsynth says, annoyed by Slagradislaun's arrogance.

"It's just that I've traveled all around and have met a great number of people and I've never heard of them. I wasn't saying it is a lie." Slagradislaun is apologetic.

"They are a rare race. There are few left and they seldom associate with the rest of us." Dervile continues, ignoring the argument, "Some Darists have the ability to slide from place to place through time, as you saw Eclant do."

Both Larsynth and Slagradislaun give Dervile their full attention.

"The Darists have long been friends to the NecroSights. They helped a great deal in our fight to stay free, often bringing words of warning to our kind to help us stay well-hidden when we may have been found out. Once they slide in they have a few short moments until they are pulled back through." Dervile continues.

"How does it all work?" Larsynth is curious.

"I'm not really sure. All I know is that it takes a great deal of concentration. You have to know where and when you are going by focusing on a specific person who you know is there at the time. Which means he somehow knows I will be here, now and he came to tell me something about Zulbarg and the dragons. I can't imagine what that would be about. We've been through there a few times but it is a small kingdom with little trade. I've certainly heard about the dragons but as far as I know they have never bothered the kingdom."

"He mentioned two names, do you remember? Lonar and Neras, I think." Slagradislaun interjects.

"Yes, that's right. They must be dragons, I guess." Larsynth adds.

"Well, I suppose so. Or maybe they are also trying to help the dragons. The problem is, how are we ever going to find them? Where are they? What do they look like? Are they expecting us?" The task is overwhelming to Dervile.

"Wait," interrupts Slagradislaun, "are we really talking about doing this? Are we heading off to Zulbarg in search of a couple of- who knows what- that we've never met and know nothing of in order to somehow help some reclusive dragons in the middle of a century's long war?"

He has to admit that with it all laid out like that the whole thing is rather a mental proposition. Yet, Dervile knows Eclant and what is more, he trusts him implicitly.

"Sure, why not?" Larsynth breaks through.

Her eyes gleam at the mere thought of what she has convinced herself could be an amazing adventure.

"Slagradislaun isn't wrong, Lars. We do need to think about this a bit more. At the least we need a plan of some sort."

"I think the plan for now is to start off in that direction." Slagradislaun points to the East. "That is, if we're doing this."

He would not mind getting a little distance between himself and his people who live to the West. He can see the reverence shared by both Dervile and Eclant for each other. Eclant has to have some reliable information, he knows Slagradislaun's name and why he has worked so hard to seek out these two NecroSights. It would not hurt to do what he can to get on their good side. What he wants from them is no small thing after all.

The three are silent contemplating the ordeal. Dervile draws in a long, deep breath before deciding for the group,

"Well, alright. We'll make our way to Zulbarg and inquire along the way about the two mentioned by Eclant. Hopefully, someone will be able to direct us to them. Or Eclant will again find us and fill us in a bit more. Lonar and Neras, I guess we'll be on our way. I'm still not sure what use we can be..."

Slagradislaun pulls his arms back grabbing for the daggers hanging from his hips. He yanks them both from their resting place. Raising his arms above his head as he twists his body around starting with his torso, his hips quick to follow. He forms an "X" with the daggers as his blades ring out a loud tinging sound. Blinking into sight there is a similar looking person with a large sword lifted high above his head trying to bring it down on Slagradislaun. Both Dervile and Larsynth jump at the rush of activity.

"You'll never succeed, Slagradislaun!" the assailant snarls.

Slagradislaun's elbows and knees bend as he absorbs his attacker's blow. He then pushes all of his strength forward, extending his arms and sending the foe staggering backward. Slagradislaun lunges forward, pulling his right elbow in close to his body and turning so that the man will take the full force of his body weight as he propels himself in fury. Dust flies up from the ground as his aggressor lands flat on his back.

The air becomes cold, sending a chill through Larsynth and her father. Both of them glance toward each other smelling the final blow that is about to come. The black smoke begins to gather to perform for the NecroSights a death scene.

Twelve

NERAS LOOKS DIRECTLY INTO Lonar's face. He is scanning it but he does not know for what. Lonar stops screaming to the other dragon's below. He stares, stunned at this tiny dragon. He has never seen one so small before. As the two are mesmerized with each other it is apparent that neither is sure what to do next. They make no attempt to harm the other. The dragons below continue yelling directions to Neras, but he blocks out their words. There is something about Lonar, he cannot place what it is, but Neras does not fear him nor does he see any great evil in him. All he sees when he looks into Lonar's face is pain, sorrow and loss. Lonar, too, is trying to read Neras' face, as a born fighter he knows that most often you can tell what a dragon's next move is going to be if you pay close enough attention to his eyes. Lonar sees no evidence that this dragon has the faintest idea of what to do with him. He knows he has never seen Neras before in any battles, he would have remembered him if not by his size then certainly by his color. Lonar is trying to stay focused on the situation at hand but wonders at this peculiar little dragon's amazing blue color. The stare down is broken as one of the largest and scariest dragons below, Veralke, bellows with his deep voice to Neras,

"Kill him or bring him down to us if you are unable."

A sharp pang of guilt and anger shoots through Neras as he turns his head to look at the crowd below. Lonar is surprised by such a careless move. A true fighter would know better than to ever turn his gaze from his opponent. More surprising, is that Lonar does not take advantage of this momentary lapse in his foe's judgment. Instead, he watches the dragon's face. He has never seen an expression of such emotion on a dragon before. Neras looks long and hard at his kin, inhales and closes his eyes. He cannot bear to watch their faces for another moment. His head turns back to Lonar whose heart drops realizing that he has made a terrible mistake in judgment by allowing the dragon that time without taking action. Two large claws wrap themselves as far around him as they can reach, pinning his arms to his sides before he has time to react. He begins to struggle to break free. Lonar has not noticed that the dragon has taken flight and is actually moving the two of them away from the crowd. They are flying through the large tunnels of the cave, back tracking the path Lonar had taken to face his life-long foes. But this is not what Lonar had expected flying would be like. They are crashing off the walls all along the path as they go. He has watched many dragons fly before and they are far more graceful than this. He thinks that the dragon is beating him about but it is clear that his captor is taking as much of the bashing as he is. Once they break through the entrance to the cave into the sunlight Lonar stops his struggle and tries to look into Neras' eyes for some clue as to what this dragon has in store for him. He wonders at the strange expression that creeps across the face of his enemy.

Flying in the sunlight for the first time, Neras is bombarded with new sensations. The warmth is welcome and comforting but the brightness is harsh and uncomfortable. He closes his eyes tight in defense as he flies higher and higher above the tree tops in order to get as close to the hotness as he can. The pain from the less than graceful flight through the tunnels is falling away the more he advances upward. He knows that something is wrong. His head feels strange, everything is spinning and he is not able to continue to glide in a straight line. He tries in vain to fix his flight path but is not able to overcome his lightheadedness. He is plummeting toward the ground out of control. Lonar can tell that Neras is not familiar with flying; his people have studied the way the dragons fly in hopes of developing weapons which will eliminate that particular advantage. He has never seen a dragon have this much difficulty in the sky not even those that have been recently injured. As far as Lonar can tell, Neras is gliding when he should have been flapping. They are going down and need to lift back up so that he can right himself.

"Flap, flap," Lonar yells.

Neras flaps his wings in a panic but nothing helps, his head is too clouded by the pain that has come rushing back. As they continue to plunge toward the ground Neras feels a sharp stinging in his tail followed by hundreds of claws scratching at him. They start at the tip of his tail and scrap their way up his body. The other dragons have come after him. They have caught him and are going to tear him apart in midair. He hears Lonar screaming at him from inside his fists which he has instinctually pulled closer to his own body for protection. He is a mother clutching her baby to its chest. Neras opens his eyes and attempts to yank his tail away from his attackers. He realizes that the scratching is in fact coming from the branches of the trees as they fell. He pulls himself into a ball allowing his side to take the most of the abuse while keeping Lonar surrounded and safe. Neras hits the ground with enough force to make the trees around him tremble. He lays on his side stunned. He rolls on to his back, pushing his claws containing Lonar into the air so as to keep him from striking the ground. He releases his tight grip on Lonar, careful not to drop him. A leaf floats down resting itself on the tip of Neras' nose, in stark contrast to the violent fall the pair has encountered. He lets it lay there as he drops his head to the rough earth and moans in pain. Lonar wiggles free from the dragon's claws and drops down to the ground silently. In a daze, he looks himself over, content that he is fine. His mind races with thoughts of what to do next. What just happened and why? What had the dragon been thinking? Should he run? Should he kill the dragon? He looks over at the little creature lying flat on its back with a single leaf perched on its nose. It is such a pathetic sight that Lonar cannot help but snicker a little.

Thirteen

"**I** FAIL TO SEE THE HUMOR in our predicament, sir." Neras retorts at the sound of Lonar laughing.

"*Our* predicament?" Lonar says, trying not to sound bitter.

It has become clear to him that Neras has no intention of killing him or he would have done so by now.

"Well, the way I see it, you are the last of your kind and right now I am feeling a bit the same. My kin will never forgive me for what I did. As such, it sounds like we are in this together."

"In what?"

"It is evident to me that there is something strange going on here." Neras explains.

He gives out a quick snort of fire from his nostrils incinerating the leaf from his nose. He fumbles about struggling to lift himself up from his landing spot. He cocks his head to the left examining Lonar. He looks up at Neras. Standing side by side the top of Lonar's head comes to the top of Neras' shoulders whereas he barely comes to the top of the knee of the other dragons he has fought. Neras is uncomfortable trying to talk to Lonar from that angle. Bending his knees, he falls backward on to the ground with a loud thud. He reaches out with the same claws that held Lonar safe and offers him to do the same. Lonar shakes his head not wanting to sit.

"Yeah, you saved my life. We're enemies. That's what's strange here."

"But why are we enemies? The things you were shouting up there make no sense. For someone in so desperate a situation to lie would be highly illogical." Neras says more to himself than to Lonar.

"Your people killed my entire village. Look, I don't know what's going on with you but I can't see us being in anything together," the rage is building up.

"If you aren't at least willing to try to talk to me than what point is there to me saving you?" Neras scans the area to be sure they have not been followed.

"I meant what I said, I will die defending the people of Zulbarg. So, don't look that direction." Lonar believes that Neras is threatening the kingdom as he unknowingly turns his head toward it.

"I wasn't looking at anything. I want to be sure that we're alone." Neras has never dealt with anyone aside from his own people and is losing patience with Lonar's unwillingness or inability to stay on track with the conversation.

"I am growing angry with this game." Lonar screams lifting his broad sword above his head.

"Game!?" Yells Neras, "you'd be dead if not for me. If that is what you desire, I can make it so."

Certain that they are getting nowhere Neras takes a deep breath, filling his lungs. Lonar drops down and rolls to his right behind a bush as Neras releases the hot flames.

The leaves of the bush crackle and glow red. The burning smell overwhelms Lonar. The memory of his home makes his heart ache. He does not care if the dragon kills him. He does not care about honor or vows or anything related to Zulbarg or King Cryptis. All he wants is his family. Lonar stands up, he knows if he stays there and waits the dragon will wind up again and it will all be over. He closes his eyes awaiting his final moment.

"AAAGGGG!" Not again! Will you kindly please?" The oddly familiar voice calls out.

Neras stops his fiery blast yelling, "Who are you? What are you doing?"

Lonar peeks his head out from around what remains of the shrub. He is unable to stifle his laugh when he sees the crazy old man from the town perched atop the dragon's snout directly behind his nostrils as Neras looks cross eyed at the inexplicable intruder.

"Yes, sorry. I seem to be more focused than ever today." Explains Eclant as he climbs off of Neras. He takes a deep bend as he introduces himself.

"Eclant here. As you no doubt have guessed I am a Darist."

"No doubt," replies Neras sarcastically.

"So, this is our first meeting, Neras?" Eclant asks.

"Yes, I…Wait, how do you know my name?"

"He does that." Lonar answers stepping out from behind his hiding spot.

"Ah, my friend, how are you?" Eclant bows toward Lonar.

"Just glad I wasn't the one you landed on this time."

"I'd think." Eclant laughs.

"You remember, the last time when you landed on me?" Lonar begins to explain.

"Yes, yes." Eclant says rubbing is leg smiling. "No bother, we have more important things to discuss and little time. Soon, Dervile, Slag and Larsynth will be here, I do hope. I can give you the part of the story that neither of you has, you must piece the rest together yourselves. I will not have time."

"What?" Neras begins but Eclant continues on speaking as quickly as he can.

"Now, you both must listen closely and don't interrupt me. The ancient King of Zulbarg thought the Gragin were too easily able to conquer his kingdom. There were always few but you are a powerful clan. At least you were, I'm sorry friend." Eclant's eyes shoot down in sincere sorrow. Remembering the importance of his story though, he continues, "Therefore, he brought the dragons here to take care of the threat. Sharsin never touched the Gem of C'Vard." He insists looking back and forth between the two enemies.

"The Gem instills fear in people. It makes them believe that everything around them can turn into something evil or harmful, even the most benign thing like, water." Eclant says pointing to the pond in the distance. "It can make them think that it is poison. It is powerful and dangerous but it is not what holds your people here." Eclant says pointedly at Neras. "My time nearly is up. Tell each other your story. Don't trust the King and talk---"

As quickly as he appeared, he is gone. Lonar and Neras stare at each other considering what happened.

"Okay, so who is Sharsin?" Neras asks.

"What? Everyone knows the story of Sharsin."

"I wouldn't say everybody. I have never heard of this person."

"Sharsin."

Lonar is getting irritated by Neras, convinced that he surely knows the story of Sharsin.

"She is the old Gragin woman that entered the Dragon cave and was tormented for 10 days. She kept her word and only told the merchant about the cave when he tricked her. The dragon's vowed death to all the people of Zulbarg for her mistake. So, since then we, the Gragin, have defended the kingdom." Lonar sadly looks to the ground adding, "We did until all my people were slaughtered."

"You defend the people of Zulbarg? That isn't how I heard it."

"Then tell me," Lonar says calming some as he can tell that Neras is not playing with him. "How did you hear it?"

"According to dragon lore the Gragin stole a precious Gem from our treasury back in the homeland. They brought the Gem of C'Vard here to Zulbarg and hope use it to take over the kingdom."

"What?" Lonar jumps to his feet in anger. "Never."

Neras waves his claw to indicate for him to settle down.

"Yes, it has become clear to me that the story I was told from a hatchling is not likely true. However, I don't believe that my kin are
aware of the inconsistency."

Lonar understands what Neras means but the idea that all these years of battling each other has been over a lie is beyond anything he can comprehend. Then something Neras has said strikes him,

"Homeland? You mean somewhere else?"

Neras shakes his head, "Yes, this place is far too cold for us dragons. We are from much farther north in a place named, Narcor."

"I don't know of my people ever living anywhere else but here, from the beginning of time." Lonar considers.

"We are told from hatchings that we, the dragon, have been the keepers of the great treasures of Dabrilas. We guard the things that are too precious for anyone to actually possess."

"Like the Gem of C'Vard?"

"Right." Neras confirms scrutinizing Lonar's face for any sign of recognition of the object. "The Gem is powerful and, as we are told, the Gragin stole it from our protection and brought it to this land."

"This Gem controls people? How is that possible?" Lonar wonders out loud.

"I don't know." Neras admits.

Lonar recalls Neras' claim that it is, in actuality, the dragon who are protecting the people of Zulbarg from the Gragin and not the other way around.

"And you think the Gragin are going to use it to take over the kingdom of Zulbarg? That doesn't make sense. We're not outcasts from the city. I myself have been there twice."

He shudders at the memory of his leisurely trip home and his culpability in not being expedient enough to save his kinsmen. He paces back and forth as the two try to make sense of everything. Neras shrugs his shoulders, not having an answer.

"All I know is that the dragons are dying. We must be closer to the sun. This climate is too cold for our kind. It's making our offspring born...wrong."

Neras' head drops in shame. Lonar knows immediately that he is talking about himself. Lonar has seen many dragons throughout his life but has never before seen one so small or so brilliant a color. He knows that such a colored dragon is certainly in more danger because it must be impossible to hide or blend in to its surrounding which is imperative for survival. Although his color is certainly considered a defect; Lonar cannot help but admire the absolute beauty of it.

"Soon, I fear, we will not be able to have any offspring at all." Neras laments.

"Why haven't you gone home then?" Lonar asks expecting that he already knows the answer.

It is the same reason his people never abandoned their village even as the attacks became more relentless. He realizes he is looking at the reason the raids have grown so much more ferocious and frequent.

"We can't. We are bound to this awful place by King Cryptis."

This is not the answer Lonar had expected.

"What do you mean by *bound*? Bound by honor"

"No, I mean physically bound. We're not able to return to our home until we restore the Gem of C'Vard to the King."

"Return? I thought you said those Gems and treasures are under the care of the dragon because they are too powerful for a person to possess. How does the King demand it from you?"

"When the Gem of C'Vard was first stolen from us the then King of Zulbarg came to my kin and revealed that he knew it had been removed and where it was hidden. He promised that he'd do everything in his power to prevent our dishonor from becoming known to all. So, an agreement was forged. The King will tell no living soul of our misfortune and in return, while we seek out the Gem in Dabrilas we will make our base here in these caves. That way we can protect Zulbarg from those who he believed intend to use it on them."

"The Gragin" Lonar finishes what Neras was going to say.

"Correct. But that crooked liar tricked us. When the last of the original party from Narcor crossed through the portal they became physically bound to this place. None have been able to return."

"Until the time that the Gem is discovered are returned?" Lonar speculates.

"That's what we've always believed." Neras concurs.

"But Eclant said that it isn't the Gem that binds you here?"

"No. In that case, I don't know what it is that holds us here. A spell or another object."

"The ancient King of Zulbarg made this agreement?"

"Yes, and it has been upheld by every King since then including King Cryptis." Neras continues.

"King Cryptis," Lonar echoes, brows furrowed. "I have just been to see him. I couldn't understand why he acted in such a strange manner."

"You have been to see the King? I don't understand. How did you manage that? Surely, his guardsmen would strike you dead on sight."

Neras exclaims in shock.

Lonar is not sure how to take that comment at first but decides it was not meant as an insult.

"I went to see him to ask for reinforcements. There being but only a few of my people left to fight..." he trails off realizing how little sense this is all starting to make.

"So, the King *is* a friend of the Gragin? This can't be. He has kept us here all the years in the guise of needing protection from your clan."

"Sounds more like blackmail to me," Lonar retorts.

Neras shakes his head in agreement.

"So, let me try to get all of this mess straight." Neras begins

"Best of luck to you," Lonar allows. He sits across from the contemplative beast.

Fourteen

"A T THE BEGINNING OF TIME the dragon lived in Narcor." Neras says firm in that detail. "And where did the Gragin live?" he asks trying to get every detail.

"Here, in Dabrilas, as far as I know. I've never heard of Narcor. I don't think my people have ever been from anywhere but here. So, I don't know how or why they would have gone to Narcor to steel anything." Lonar tries not to get defensive.

"No, I doubt your ancestors have ever lived in our world. The heat would not be kind to creatures such as yourself." Neras concludes.

Lonar had not considered that as he sees the dragon as a type of beast, to a dragon he is nothing more than a form of creature. He now sees Neras as being fair minded and can tell that he is trying to get to the truth without ulterior motives of his own.

"Okay," Neras continues. "Shortly after the beginning of time *someone* took the Gem of C'Vard from the dragon treasury in Narcor. We now know that this Gem is used to control people."

Lonar looks to the pond seeing only beauty, nothing harmful.

"That sounds more like a loss of control."

"Yes, in the most terrible way." Neras agrees also looking toward the pond.

Wanting to get back to the overall picture, Lonar tries to get Neras back on track,

"Okay, so *someone* stole the Gem from the dragon treasury in Narcor."

"Right, the Gem is missing." Neras verifies retuning to the convoluted history. "For several nights my people searched in vain for it.".

"Is this where the ancient King comes in?" Lonar asks.

"Yes, in fact, it is. I believe it was a full two cycles before he came to Narcor. He met with the council of elders," Neras recounts. He tries to stop his mind from flashing back to his most recent encounter with the council.

"Um, oh yeah," Neras waves away the memory; "he met with the council and told them that he had conclusive information on the whereabouts of the Gem. That a band of fighters living outside his city walls had taken up permanent camp and he feared that they will use the Gem on his people."

"This is actually making a little sense. About that time, which is when the story of Sharsin takes place, is when the King's proxy reached out to the Gragin to be protectors of the Kingdom of Zulbarg. But we were to protect the kingdom from the dragons. Which we felt was our duty as we had angered them."

"Had you?" Neras asks. "Isn't it possible that there is no Sharsin? Within no more than a full cycle my people had taken up residency in those caves. Had any Gragin seen a dragon before that time?"

"As the story goes, Sharsin didn't know the dragon existed before then. She was innocently walking through the forest and into a cave."

The most important line from the Retelling springs into his head, "*Which she has every right to do.*"

Neras looks at Lonar, "so it wouldn't have been at all unusual up until this point for a Gragin to go into the cave?"

"No, but that certainly wouldn't have been true if the dragon were already there."

"It sounds like both our stories are right." Neras considers.

"And wrong." Lonar points out.

"Yes. The dragon came to this area in search for our Gem at the, as you put it, blackmailing of the King. Before Sharsin went into the cave."

"Right, the Gem was already missing."

"But the King claimed that the Gragin were new to this area, which is what caused him fear."

"I assure you, my people have been here for a long time. Since we saved the kingdom during the siege of Jalib."

"When was that?"

"About one thousand cycles or more ago, I'd guess. We have been here ever since then."

"Yes, I believe you have. Have the Gragin always been superior fighters?"

"As it is told," Lonar confirms.

"Umm," Neras thinks, trying to put the pieces together, "Why would the king blame the Gragin? How did he know that the Gem had been stolen?"

"How did the King know?" Lonar is confused. "I can't work out that part of it."

"Me either, but I am confident that both our ancestors were wronged. That all this fighting began under false pretenses." Neras bows his head, "That you should not have to be the last one of your kin left."

Lonar can hear the sorrow in Neras' voice.

"Eclant was right to warn us against trusting the King. Of this, I am certain. If he has a relationship with the dragon and the Gragin then, he is lying to both. When I asked for reinforcements, telling him that most of my people have been wiped out he did not show any interest. I warned him that we can no longer protect the kingdom from the dragon but it didn't concern him in the least."

"Because he knows the dragon will never attack the city. The dragon only care about getting back our Gem."

"That isn't true," Lonar corrects, "You want to get back to Narcor. Which you believe requires getting back your Gem and in the meantime, in order to keep your secret safe..."

"We must defend the kingdom of Zulbarg."

"Indeed." Lonar nods.

"The Gem of C'Vard isn't in the hands of the Gragin at all." Neras proclaims. "The King told us that to bring us here."

"And keep you here," Lonar adds.

"Looking for something we will never find and killing off a people that could someday, become a threat to Zulbarg." Neras lifts his head to the sky understanding.

"With the added bonus of having the Gragin here also in case any other King of the realm decides to attack."

"But the Gem, which certainly was taken from us? What of it?"

"The King really does have that piece of information. How could he know?" Lonar wonders.

"Do you think it's possible?... Does the King have it? Is that who took it all along?" Neras hypothesizes.

"It certainly is possible but why then be the one to alert the dragon?" Lonar asks.

"That's easy. He'd be the last person we'd suspect then. Add to that his fear that someone else could find out that he has it. Who better to protect him than the dragon?" Neras becomes furious now, "Do you think this all can be possible?"

"So, the King has the Gem of C'Vard." Lonar concludes.

"I don't know but it's most probable." Neras agrees.

Lonar jumps to his feet. "I intend to find out. If the King does have the Gem then he's using it to control his people."

"Yes, I believe he does." Neras can come to no other logical conclusion. "I also believe that the ancient King that first came to the dragon is the one who stole it in the first place. He used it on the dragon to trick us into coming to this place. We escorted him here, which is when he began using it on his own people. The rest was lies to get us here."

"And so the secret has been passed from King to King."

"Now to King Cryptis." Neras revels in the awareness.

"We must get it from him; we have to stop him from using it." Lonar declares with certainty and passion.

"Yes, of course, this cannot continue. But how?" Neras is doubtful.

"Go, tell your people. The dragon can easily take over the city and find it. That's what they have been doing to my village for centuries. Certainly, the people of Zulbarg will be no match---" As he hears himself he stops mid-sentence. "No, the people cannot be harmed."

"Agreed. We will have to be more covert in our attempts to regain control of the Gem and we don't know if he's keeping it in the castle." Neras considers. "Sadly, I don't think my people will be of any help. They'll never believe any of this."

"We can't do this alone." Lonar argues.

"If I were the last of the dragon and it was the Gragin we needed to turn to right now, how do you think they would react?"

Lonar ponders it.

"Then, it's up to us," he says with understanding.

"So, all we have to do is break in to the castle, steel the Gem, remove its power over the people of Zulbarg and find a way to return my people to Narcor. Sounds like fun." Neras jokes, looking around the forest.

"Say, you don't happen to know where we are? Or at least which direction the castle is from here; do you Gragin?" Neras asks.

"My name is Lonar and you've never been outside the cave before have you?"

"Well, not really, no."

"Not really? What does that mean?" Lonar asks.

"Okay then, no, I haven't...been outside the cave...before...ever."

"And you don't know how to fly either?"

"Well, I thought I did." Neras smiles.

"Oh, this *is* going to be fun." Lonar points to the way of the castle as the odd pair head off to meet their destiny, together.

Fifteen

THE RANCID STINK OVERTAKES HER; Larsynth's stomach drops and twists itself until she cannot catch her breath. Her heart is being squeezed by the cold as the awful sight plays out in front of her. The parts are being enacted by the chilling black smoke. She has been witness to these events more than a few times in her life but this is the first time she has ever experienced such panic observing death's performance. The dark smoke, in the visage of Slagradislaun, falls to the ground pulling the dagger from his heart.

Larsynth cries out, "SLAG, NO!"

Her insides are trying to dash forward to him to do something, anything to stop this from happening but her body refuses to move. There she stands in absolute horror. Normally, this would be nothing more than a game to her; can she prevent death from obtaining the prize it sought? This particular round of the unending sport between the two would have been exceedingly easy for Larsynth to interfere with and change course.

She should be able to see all the ways to foil Slagradislaun's impeding murder; as the enemy lays sprawled on the ground reaching for the dagger from his boot she could snatch it from his hand as he lifts it toward Slagradislaun. She could run and push Slagradislaun out of the way making him land on his side on the ground instead of his current trajectory forward to his awaiting fate. She should be able to think of any number of creative yet effective ways to prevent this specific death but none come to her.

She knows that even if they did it would be no use as her body continues to defy and betray her.

Dervile, on the other hand, springs to action as soon as he sees the smoke version of Slagradislaun's assailant reach toward his boot for the dagger. He rushes over to the spot and with one quick thwack of his walking stick he raps the man's hand hard enough to make the small knife go flying from his grasp.

Out of the corner of his eye, Slagradislaun sees the old man running toward him but is not sure what to make of it until the glint of the blade temporarily blinds him as it flies across the front of the other Franeglian's body and onto the ground beside them. Slagradislaun does not hesitate as he twirls the daggers in his hands pointing the sharp blades downward toward his adversary. The tips slid into the body of his attacker. He stops struggling. The trickling of green blood turns to a steady leak. Slagradislaun closes his eyes in disgust; disgust at the sight of the now dead body of someone who should have been his friend, possibly a kinsman of his.

His people have no trouble with killing and has little or no remorse when a life is taken. He does not share this gruesome way of thinking. Every life he takes, from the time he was first taught how to wield his daggers, makes him ill. Even when he kills for nourishment he thanks the creature for its sacrifice so that he may have sustenance. He believes that he has an obligation to the lowliest of animals that he has consumed that it is his sacred duty to live a life worthy of what they have given to him. Surveying this body, he becomes morose. His temper rises up in his chest, he is going to explode. Slagradislaun turns to Dervile and roars at the kindly old man who saved his life,

"THIS," he screams pointing to the corpse soaked through in its own blood, "This is why I need you!"

Dervile raises his hand, palm up to Slagradislaun trying to calm him, "I know."

"This HAS to stop. They can't continue like this." He drops his daggers and falls to his knees. "They know what I'm trying to do and they are going to keep coming after me. I don't want to put the two of you in danger but I have no other choice."

"Considering the circumstances, you're right to come. I'm glad you found us and we won't give up until we succeed." Dervile reassures him.

He walks over to Slagradislaun and clutches the man's quivering shoulder.

"You're obviously a good and brave young man. The three of us will keep each other safe."

He looks to his beloved daughter hoping his face is not betraying him.

Larsynth watches her dad comfort this stranger as if he was his own son. They have a mutual understanding of something to which she is not privy. She wants to insist on being let in on whatever it is that these two are thinking, but it is clear that this is not the time. She respects the moment that they are having. She stands in silent reverence of the two men. Slagradislaun, who she had previously thought of as the arrogant, suspicious outsider, now makes her heart ache for him. Seeing his body hunched over shaking, his voice cracking with emotion and his eyes pleading for help, she feels from deep inside her soul that she and her father will do, must do, and HAVE to do anything it takes to help him. Her father agrees.

"Come now, we need to be on our way. He may not be alone." Dervile says, looking around.

Slagradislaun reaches for his daggers. His face drops more as he looks at the green liquid dripping from them. He wipes the blades clean in the grass before returning them to the sheaths on his hips. He stands up and turns to Larsynth looking her in the eye for the first time since the attack began. He has been avoiding seeing what she might think of him after witnessing these events, how she might fear him or hate him for putting her life and her father's life in danger. He would not blame her for either. His heart skips a beat when he sees the softness in her expression. What is registering on her face is not anger or horror but something different.

Sixteen

NERAS STOPS AT THE EDGE of the forest of Hugret looking down at the destroyed village. Pangs of guilt cut through him. He wants to stop Lonar from seeing this sad view.

"Is there any another way? This path is going to be hard to traverse." He lies.

"No, it should be fine." Lonar replies unaware of what Neras is trying to do.

"I just came up this way…"

Lonar pauses when he reaches the precipice where Neras is waiting. He does not see the burned out buildings or the toppled trading stalls. To Lonar, all that remains are the dead bodies of his loved ones. He sees the many centuries worth of his ancestors that have gone before him and the descendants that were to come after but that now never will. He sees his brothers, nieces, cousins, parents and grandparents. He sees his friends and those dearest to him, all in a heap like discarded rubbish. The sight takes his breath away.

He jerks when he feels the weight of Neras' claw. Although it is much smaller than any other dragon claw it is still startling.

Lonar imagines himself turning on the unsuspecting dragon and plunging his broad sword straight into his heart. Then cutting off his little head and returning to the cave with his trophy. As much hatred as he has for the dragons after being raised with nothing but tales of their nefarious crimes against his people, he has no such animosity toward Neras. Lonar swallows his anger but there is nothing he can do about the tears. He wipes his eyes blinking away the fluid distorting his view.

"I'm sorry." Neras pulls away from Lonar noticing his body tense up at his touch. "For all of it."

"You've got to be kidding me." Lonar says in disbelief.

Neras bows his head in respect, "No... really... I, I know our people have been taught nothing but hatred and bitterness toward the other. But truly I am sorry for---"

"No, I believe *that*. It's THAT I can't believe." Lonar exclaims pointing to the lanky figure in the village.

The long white hair blowing in the wind is unmistakable. That crazy old man is back.

"Well, that's unexpected." Neras jolts upright at the sight of the strange man. "What's he doing down there? He'll probably disappear before we get to him."

"Yeah? How will we ever manage to be confused but the randomness that comes out of his mouth this time?" Lonar mocks.

"Shall I try to fly down to him?"

"It's your funeral but I'll take the long way if you don't mind."

"Oh, no, I understand perfectly." Neras takes a few long strides backward before turning to Lonar and giving him a "here goes nothing" grin.

He runs forward to the cliff's edge with all the speed he can muster before throwing himself off. Lonar grimaces and closes his eyes not wanting to see the inevitable crash of his new partner.

"AAAAHHHHHH!" Is all he hears before the unmistakable loud thudding sound of a dragon not flying.

Neras grabs for every tree, rock and spec of dirt on his way careening down the side of the ledge. He is hoping something, anything will slow down his descent. As he rolls head over tail all he sees is dirt, trees, sky followed by more dirt, trees, sky. The pattern continues his whole trip. Lonar breaks out into a dash down the winding path calling out to Neras every few seconds.

"I'm coming... you're fine...everything's alright!"

He does not know why he keeps lying but he figures it is the thing you say in a situation like this. He marvels that he is in a situation like this at all.

Neras is still in a ball when his journey ends. Letting out a little puff of smoke he exhales and lays out flat on his back. He remains still; he looks up at the sky trying to get the ground to stop moving beneath him. He reaches back with both claws grabbing at the dirt to make sure he does not fall off.

"That was something." Lonar smirks trying not to laugh seeing that Neras is unscathed from his ordeal.

"Ugh, well, I was trying to lighten the mood. Whatever it takes to make you smile." Neras replies relieved to see Lonar bounding toward him.

"Oh my, that was some tumbling routine." Eclant claps getting to the two. "My name is Eclant." He introduces himself reaching out his hand to Lonar as Neras struggles to get himself off of the ground.

Lonar isn't sure what to do. He reaches out his hand. "Yes, I know... we've met... three times."

"Yes, is that so? Well, I look forward to meeting you again for the first time then. And you my fine entertainer," he turns to Neras, "have we met?"

"Yes, earlier today in fact."

"Ah, excellent, well, okay then. As you're all caught up with me how about if you catch me up?"

Neras and Lonar look at each other for some explanation as to what is going on and what they should do.

"I don't always do things in the same order as everyone else" Eclant tries to clarify, sensing their confusion.

"How are you still here for so long?" Neras questions out loud looking the man over.

"Oh, yes, of course, you've only met me during a slide. Well, it's simple. I'm here because... well, I'm here. This is my normal timeline." Eclant looks at both of them hoping for some sign of understanding but finding none. "When you've met me before it was me from the future sliding back in time. Probably to tell you something important or warn you."

"You didn't really do either the first two times we met." Lonar argues.

"No one can get it right all the time. I'd like to see you try it yourself and see if you do any better." Eclant defends himself.

"Okay, okay" Lonar concedes. "So, if you don't know who we are I guess we're going to have to start at the beginning and tell you everything, that's happening or happened or will happen, I think. Maybe. I'm really not sure where to start now that I think of it."

"The beginning, that will be refreshing, yes, let's try that." Eclant agrees.

Seventeen

"THE SOONER WE HEAD OUT the faster we can put some distance between us and those hunting you." Dervile points out to Slagradislaun.

"My own people, that's who is hunting me." Slagradislaun's shoulders slump.

"They'd never suspect you'd be going to Zulbarg." Dervile guesses.

"No, no one really ever goes to Zulbarg. There isn't much reason to and the people there are a little ...odd." Slagradislaun agrees.

"True, there is something about them that is a bit unsettling. I've always thought so but could never really put my finger on what it is. They are not unfriendly per se but they don't care for outsiders much. They are more than willing to participate in trade but there really is not much trading to be done with them. I always feel unwelcome when I'm in the kingdom."

Dervile has not noticed that the other two are already making their way up the path to the East. It is probably the first time he has ever put into words his nagging feelings about the place. It is something everyone who has ever visited Zulbarg has felt on some level or another but is rarely ever able to explain. Dervile does about as good of a job describing it as anyone before him ever has. He rushes to catch up to Larsynth and Slagradislaun.

"Do you think it might be time for you and Dad to let me in on what's going on? Why you've come to us and what it is you want our help with? Why are your own people trying to kill you?"

Larsynth wants to leave Slagradislaun alone after all that she has seen, but for her own peace of mind she needs more explanation of what is going on. She cannot understand why he was saying those things to her father or to comprehend her father's reaction to it.

Dervile catches up to the two of them in time to hear his daughter's inquiries. His instinct is to shoot her a look of warning to let it be but on further consideration he decides he is wrong. His daughter will forever be his little girl but the truth of the matter is, she is actually a rather grown young woman. If this man is going to be traveling with them, does not she have every right to a full understanding of the situation? If they are going to help him then there is a certain amount of risk that is going to be an ever present part of their lives. He cannot guarantee that he will be able to keep it from her. Not letting her have all of the information may actually put her more in danger than hiding it from her. His heart aches at the sad realization that he is acknowledging that his baby girl is grown and that he cannot protect her from every bad thing in the world. There are forces outside of his control when it comes to Larsynth. The unhappy realization brings tears to his eyes and a weakness in his knees.

Dervile concludes that even in the face of his baby girl's rapid transition to womanhood, when it comes down to it, this is not his story to tell. It is up to Slagradislaun. He has to be the one to decide to share the truth about who he is, his people, what they are and his plan to stop them. Dervile will take it from there and inform Larsynth of what their role in all of this is but not until Slagradislaun is ready to share his side. The look on the young man's face tells Dervile that he is ashamed and fearful, though he fights hard to hide it. Now it not the time.

The silence between the three of them hangs on every drop of atmosphere. They breathe it in deep and exhale it out. There is no tension, it is flat, death-like silence. It not the kind that is created when someone is hard at work on something that requires a great deal of concentration. This is the silence of avoidance.

The road before them is empty, easy and flat. The land around them now is nothing more than wide open plains. They have no fear of being ambushed. The weather is pleasant enough that they can keep a swift pace without much trouble and the sky is clear as the stars shine down on them leading the way to the East, Zulbarg and their fate. The excitement Larsynth once felt at what she was certain was going to be a great adventure has now died down as the reality of what may be waiting for them is starting to sink in. She spent most of the journey so far trying to work out why no one is talking. She does not understand that the men are afraid that if they begin to speak, they will be helpless but to have all their secrets spill out of them unwillingly for trying to appease Larsynth.

She lets the hush wrap itself around them. She is not pouting as used to be her habit when not getting what she wanted. It is time to put aside that childish behavior. She is struggling with an internal war. She wants to be treated like an equal, instead of a fragile little thing that needs protection. Yet, she respects her father and trusts that he knows best and that when the time comes he will open up to her. When it comes to Slagradislaun, she does not mind so much that he is trying to protect her because she has the desire to do the same for him. Right now, she senses that not pestering him is the best thing she can do for him. His emotions after killing that man had boiled over so surprisingly that she believes that he probably needs a little time to get himself back together before talking to her about anything. The rest of the day will be a quiet one as each person spends this part of the journey alone within themselves walking together down their path.

Slagradislaun closes his eyes breathing in the new day and exhaling out the old one. It is nice to expel the rot that had been infesting him since yesterday's events. He looks around at the wide open plain, knowing they have a long yet easy two days of travel ahead of them. But, the constant questioning in Larsynth's eyes is not going to go away. He was not in any state of mind to talk to her about any of it earlier. He is thankful that she let it drop for the rest of the day. He can tell that reprieve will not last. He is going to have to explain himself to her. He is not sure how to bring it up or how much he should say. He has no idea why this is so scary to him. All he has to do is open his mouth and talk but when he looks her in the eye his heart races. His thoughts are of the udder fear that absorbs him, convinced that she will think of him as one of *them*. He knows he would not be able to bear that. He has to make her see how he is different. Which is the whole reason he left everything he has known since birth, turned his back on his family and his people and began his search for NecroSights.

Every young Franeglian has heard about NecroSights; most think they are not real. They're nothing more than a story you tell a child to scare them into behaving. The oldest among them claim to have known one or two in their time but agree that there likely are few left, if any at all. When he started this pursuit he did not know what to believe. He knew that if there was one left still breathing he had to seek him out. Then he would have to do anything necessary to convince him to help. He could barely believe his luck when he found not one, but two. He felt the greatest relief when Dervile agreed to help him, knowing exactly what was being asked of him. This business with the dragons will slow things down but having a Darist on their side will make it worth the trouble. For now, he has to keep himself alive and them safe at all costs from his own kind who are not going to ever give up trying to stop them. His burden is great but he knows it is something that has to be done.

"Slag," Larsynth starts, hoping that now that everyone has had time to recover from the previous days' happenings it might be the right opportunity to find out what she and her father are getting themselves into. Also, what it is that he is so afraid of and unwilling to open up to her about.

Slagradislaun smiles, he does not mind his new nickname anymore. He remembers during his fight with the other Franeglian when she screamed out in fear for his life. The emotion in her voice was unexpected but appreciated.

"Yes, it's time." He does not make her ask. "I'm a Franeglian. We are a people from the West. You already know about our curse of OverSight." Slagradislaun begins.

"Few Franeglian will agree that it's a curse. OverSight is what makes them so formidable." Dervile interrupts.

"That's true. Franeglian are excellent fighters aside from the OverSight. We're light and nimble and are trained exclusively to be fighters from birth. We are taught nothing but how to wield these," he pulls his daggers from his hips. "And to murder. We then couple this training with the OverSight and have become nothing more than assassins and thieves." Slagradislaun continues with loathing.

Larsynth can see his hatred for his own kind in his eyes when he speaks of them.

"It's the OverSight." Dervile adds seeing the obvious question in his daughter's face. "As we, NecroSights, have an extra sight also, we are able to remove the OverSight from the Franeglian. At least that has been the belief but I don't know of anyone who has ever tried."

"If they have, they obviously haven't succeeded." Slagradislaun put in. "But there's a good reason why NecroSights may not want to help the Franeglian."

He looks at Dervile who shakes his head indicating that he does not want Slagradislaun to continue with what he was about to say.

"There was never another Franeglian willing to do away with OverSight anyway I'm sure." He changes focus. "Unlike the NecroSights it has not brought harm to my people. At least that's what they believe. I see it differently. We are the worst of the worst. We kill and steal with abandon because so many believe it's our right because of the OverSight. It is not honorable. You see, ridding the Franeglian of OverSight is best for everyone. It will keep the rest of the world safe from my people and it will keep my people from their vile ways." Slagradislaun explains.

Dervile is relieved that Slagradislaun leaves out the part that is going to upset Larsynth. She is young and does not see things as he does. When she finds out, he doubts she will agree to pay such a high price but that is for another day.

Eighteen

"WE'RE GOING TO NEED someplace to stay for now until we can come up with a plan." Neras explains to Lonar and Eclant. "We don't know for certain where the Gem is. I suggest we take a little time to do some research before we attempt to storm the castle and demand the King hand it over to us."

"That isn't a good plan at all, no, we need to stay in one place for now." Eclant agrees. "Here in this town, close to the castle, is the best spot until we know more."

"Is this going to be alright with you?" Neras is concerned for Lonar.

"Well, there isn't much left of the village and as small as you are for a dragon, I'm not sure you'd fit comfortably in one of the shacks anyway, even if they were still standing." Lonar surveys the destruction of his home once again. "There is a cave right over here though that could work for us. It's roomy and will keep us out of the elements." Lonar points to his right on the edge of the village.

"Yes, it will also do to keep the King thinking that the Gragin are gone. If he sees activity here in the city, he'll know some have survived." Eclant adds looking to the castle. "I'm afraid my sliding may not work as handily for us as I would have liked. I can't go into the castle and look around. I have to slide through time and to a specific person. I need to know when and where they will be. Once I'm there I'll have to maneuver around the guards."

"No, that won't work. I was just in the castle, its crawling with sentries. There is no way you'd be able to creep around without getting caught. There are too many of them."

"Interesting," considers Neras. "That makes me believe that perhaps we are thinking along the correct lines as to where to seek the Gem."

"Ummm," nods Eclant.

"First, come let's prepare the cave. We need to take care of our shelter and food. We can discuss our next move over a meal." Lonar walks toward the cavern.

■■■

"Well, did you see anything or anyone out of place?" Dervile asks as Larsynth and Slagradislaun return to the previously agreed upon meeting spot in the tavern.

There is a feeling that everyone in the place is watching them. He had hoped they would be able to slip in and out of town with little attention but that rarely happens in Zulbarg. Everyone takes note when someone new is around, and they watch, wary of what harm they might do.

"I didn't see anything and no one saw me." Slagradislaun replies.

"Me either. You're right about the people here though, Dad. I never felt for one moment as though I wasn't being watched as if I'm going steal something."

"Well, you do have a certain look." Slagradislaun teases, grinning at her.

"Yes, I suppose." Dervile absentmindedly mumbles clearly not paying attention to what the two are saying.

"Father! I don't---" Larsynth objects, swatting him on the arm.

"What? Oh, sorry." Dervile can see that he has missed something. "I was just thinking," he points to the Gragin settlement through the window "they may be up there."

"It's getting too dark. I'm afraid we'll have to stay here tonight and head up after morning meal." Slagradislaun concludes agreeing with Dervile.

■■■

"How is everyone this afternoon?" Eclant asks walking into the cave with a string full of fish from the small pond in the forest. "I have nourishment."

Lonar and Neras blink and stretch themselves releasing the night's sleep that does not want to give up its hold of either one of them. Eclant sits on the stone nearest to the fire and begins to clean the fish he caught. Lonar picks himself up from his makeshift bed in the dirt. He wanders over to where Eclant is sitting, grabbing a fish for himself. He too gets to work descaling one.

"I wish I could be more help but my claws don't give me as much dexterity as your hands do." Neras laments.

"You, my friend, are the most important part of the meal preparation," Lonar comforts him as Eclant hands him a freshly cleaned fish.

"Happily." Neras takes the fish, setting it on another stone before inhaling then letting out a quick cough of fire.

"I think I may have overdone this one." He apologizes tossing it back to Lonar.

Peeling off a few charred spots he reassures Neras, "Nah, it's...what is that? Does anyone else hear something?"

They all stop what they are doing and listen. The three of them jump, hurrying for the cave entrance. Lonar grabs his broad sword on the way out.

Lonar stops dead when he sees two strangers walking around the village admiring all of the destruction. He reaches his arm out to seize Neras so that they can have the advantage of surprise.

"What are you doing here my old friend!?" Eclant screams nearly at the top of his lungs rushing out to greet Dervile. Lonar and Neras jerk, still watching the outsiders suspiciously.

"Well, you're going to come and find us," Dervile explains reaching his hand out to indicate Slagradislaun and Larsynth "and tell us that our help is needed here in Zulbarg. You will briefly mention the dragons and the people fighting them?"

"And that led you up here? Excellent. You are a bright man." Eclant is pleased with both Dervile and himself. He also appreciates having someone around who understands him well enough to know when to speak in the future tense with him; it helps to avoid confusion.

"A Franeglian? I did not see you until Dervile pointed you out. That's unusual. How did this happen...? Oh my, Is it time then? No more extraordinary Sights?" He asks looking to Dervile who simply smiles back to him. "Well, let's get on with it. Neras, Lonar show yourselves. I'm going to ask the help of these people and as you can see they have agreed to assist us. The time has come to begin."

Neras and Lonar step out from the cave entrance. Larsynth cannot believe what she is seeing. She has heard tales of dragons but has never been eye to eye with one before. She expected it to be much bigger and much scarier. Nothing about this creature makes her the least bit afraid. He is not much more than the height of her father but his head is massive and his tail drags on the ground but is now curled up around his feet. She cannot stop staring at him in amazement. His skin is the most beautiful shade of sapphire that she has ever seen. She tries to remind herself that those are not the arms of a muscular man but of a beast. This is a being with long sharp teeth and blade like claws in place of hands but to her none of that is registering. All she can see as she gawks at him is something more awe inspiring than anything she has previously come across in all of her travels. More stunning than any precious stone, mountain view or starry night. She has to fight back her urge to reach out and touch him. She longs to know how his scales feel on her fingertips. Are they cold? Are they jagged? Will they cut her? She does not care. She has to know. The sensation overtakes her.

"What will he smell like?" she wonders.

Is he salty like the refreshing ocean or smoky like a cold night's warming fire? She examines his nostrils wondering if they are the source of his flame that she is heard so much about and that everyone else fears. Or does it spew forward from his mouth through those incredible white fangs? She is yearning to see for herself.

"How powerful he must be." Is all she keeps going back to in her mind. Her eyes do their best to take him in. By the time they met his she has seared every detail of his impressive physique into her mind. She notices that he is looking at her with a matching intensity, her heart jumps into her throat. She does not look away in embarrassment; she cannot make herself break the gaze between them. His large eyes are a purer hue of green than she has ever seen. More than that though, is the kindness they exude. She does not know how she can tell that but absolutely trusts that she is seeing right into his soul and she sees only goodness and compassion in it.

This is the first time Neras has seen a female human. He is studying her differently than he did Lonar. He found Lonar to be a bit of a curiosity, that was the extent of his fascination. He is not trying to figure how she works. Nor is he confused about how such a squishy outside could ever keep her alive like he did when surveying Lonar. He has already decided that human have a flawed design when it comes to survival, they are not well insulated and their skin breaks up easily. He cannot fathom such tiny and breakable bones or how they manage to keep warm at all. Dragons are thick but they still feel cold, all of the time in this atmosphere. But when he looks upon the sight of her, his thoughts turn to her appearance rather than structure. The softness of her skin, which he previously considered unsuitable for any living thing, fits her well. Though the color is a bit dull for what he is accustomed to, it is nothing short of perfection. He becomes preoccupied by the uncontrollable impulse to touch it. If he had any sensation in his legs he is sure he would be making a fool of himself. While Lonar's hair sweeps far beyond his shoulders, it is limp, falling about unimpressively. Even though Eclant's hair is white, thin and as long as Lonar's it lays in a similar way. Neras believed that is natural for human hair. Her hair, is remarkable, it flows like water down her shoulders and onto her back. It waves in the wind and beckons for you to wrap yourself up in it and sleep for all eternity. Her lips curl on the edges in a way that puts him at ease. Her face is relaxed but her eyes are intense. They are looking directly into his, past his even, he suspects. This is the first time since leaving the safety of his mountain home and the security of his people that he feels vulnerable but, still safe. Nothing about her penetrating scrutiny is uncomfortable or threatening. In fact, it is warm and affectionate. He does not look away; she is not either. This is a strong being he can sense, but a delicate one too. This dichotomy intrigues him. He is eager to get to know her so that he can confirm his beliefs.

"Don't worry, I won't let the beast harm you." Slagradislaun declares stepping between Larsynth and Neras.

"No, I don't think any harm will come to me from him." She announces as she walks forward joining the conversation between her father and Eclant. She smiles at Neras, then glances back to Slagradislaun with an appreciative grin.

"As I'm the only one aware of who or what everyone here is. I suppose I should provide for the introductions." Eclant begins. "My two companions here know all about me as does Dervile but do the two of you?" He asks looking to Slagradislaun and Larsynth.

"My dad explained a little, you're a Darist?" she asks, unsure if she has remembered the term correctly.

"Yes, my dear, I am. There are few of us around. I think about six these days. Darists have the ability to slide through time from one place to another. Yet, I cannot slide from here to there." He explains pointing to the castle in the distance. "I can slide to the castle to a different point in time, in the past, if I know someone, other than myself, is there. I have to know specifically where and when I want to travel to. It is easy to get it wrong, which I do often. I'm afraid."

Lonar chuckles.

"Now this is Lonar." Eclant continues. "We are currently in the village of his people, the Gragin." Everyone looks around acknowledging their whereabouts except for Lonar who cannot stand to see the destruction any more than he has to. "This here is Neras, he's a dragon. Well, I guess you can see that for yourselves. I suppose he might seem a bit small to you."

"Um, no, not really." Slagradislaun interjects. "I mean; I've never seen a dragon before but he looks pretty imposing to me."

"As dragons go, trust me, he's tiny." Lonar corrects.

"No offense." He looks at Neras realizing that did not come out right.

"Oh, no, none taken. It's the basic truth. I'm about a quarter of the size of most of my clan." Neras reassures Lonar. "I should probably tell you all before you ask, I'm not be able to fly like the other dragons either."

"No, I will definitely say not." Eclant laughs at the memory of the dragon tumbling down the side of the cliff upon his arrival to the village.

"I don't think it's nice to laugh at him for that." Larsynth scolds.

"Right, apologizes." Eclant straightens himself up. "Lonar and Neras need our help."

"Actually, the people of Zulbarg are the ones who need all of our help." Lonar corrects.

"Tis true, I must say. Really, that is more so true." Eclant acquiesces. "Have you many dealing with the people in the town?" Eclant looks to Dervile.

"A few times. We spent the night there last evening in fact."

"Have you ever felt that the people there are somehow…off?" Eclant pursues.

"Indeed! We were talking about that such thing last nightfall. They are a particularly suspicious group, I've found." Dervile exclaims.

"Ah, but through no fault of their own. We believe that the King has a wicked Gem that has taken ahold of their senses." Lonar adds.

"To what end?" Dervile wonders aloud.

"Control." Eclant replies. "The Gem of C'Vard is a devious little beggar that instills an overall sense of fear in the hearts of those infected. Nothing distorts reality like fear. When one is no longer able to see what the truth of a situation is, it is then that they are left wide open for another to come in and lie to them. These lies can easily lead to superstition and irrational behavior. Nothing is sweeter to a leader than a fearful flock for they are the most obedient." Eclant's words hang heavy in the air.

The others shiver at the truth he has just spoken. The most honest things ever said are the hardest to hear.

"The King has been using the Gem also as a way to create a war between the Gragin and the dragons." Lonar breaks the silence wanting to explain how all of this involves him and Neras.

"Yes." Neras continues. "Our people are the protectors of the Gem which was stolen from our land, Narcor, and brought here. We are not from Dabrilas and the time being away from our home is killing us. More dragons are being hatched wrong, like me." Neras cannot help but be ashamed. Larsynth wants to comfort him seeing how the words pain him to admit.

"We must be freed to return to Narcor or I fear the next generation may not be born at all. We were blackmailed by the King centuries ago. He lured us here to retrieve the Gem. Then he double crossed us, not allows any to return through the portal. He told us the Gragin were hiding it and planned to us it on his people."

"Which isn't true." Lonar adds.

"Agreed." Neras nods. "But I don't believe that I can convince the others of the same." He says looking back to the mountains where his fellow dragons reside.

"I now know what it is like to be the last of your kind." Lonar shakes his head in sadness. "I don't want that to happen to Neras and even though the dragons are to blame for the deaths of my family and destruction of my home." He sweeps his arms out wide indicating the devastation surrounding them. "My hatred is for the King who has done this to us, to the dragons and to his own people."

"So, you believe the Kings of Zulbarg have truly been the ones possessing the Gem and have been using it to control their people? All the while falsely bringing the dragons here to fight innocents?" Slagradislaun tries to make sense of it all. "Why?"

"The Gragin have always been a warrior tribe. Certainly, setting up camp so near to the tiny kingdom must have been threatening to the King who knows they can snatch it from him at any moment." Eclant clarifies.

"Two birds with one stone then?" Dervile spat with disgust.

"Exactly." Eclant agrees.

"So, how are they going to be a help to us and why would they want to get involved in all of this?" Lonar asks as politely as possible.

"Ah!" Eclant grins. "These are special people indeed. They may be the key to retrieving the Gem."

Nineteen

DERVILE GRABS HIS DAUGHTER'S ARM as the familiar rotten smell fills their nostrils. Both of them look from person to person waiting to see whose unlucky fate this is. The odor becomes so overwhelming that Larsynth thinks she is going to be sick. She doubles over, reaching for her stomach. The black smoke begins to appear around the feet of Lonar, Neras and Eclant.

"Everyone in the cave, NOW!" Dervile demands in a voice that makes even Larsynth jump.

Eclant is the first to heed the warning. Lonar and Neras stand in bewilderment at what the man is screaming about. They watch as he flails his arms in the air. Slagradislaun breaks their stare running toward them. He pushes Lonar with all of his strength.

"Do as he says!" Slagradislaun yells in the awestruck duo's faces.

"Now, go, now!" Larsynth regains her composer and is herself heading for the cave.

"Come, Come!" Eclant shouts in agreement motioning to everyone as they approach the cave entrance.

Lonar is pushed into the cavern by Slagradislaun. He resists the need to defend himself against the random attach by the man he has just met. Lonar does not doubt that something is happening outside the cave from the chorus of warnings going on all around him but he cannot suppose what it might be. He hears the all too familiar sound, *dragons*, the realization is a sick feeling in his guts. Considering that all the other remaining Gragin have perished in the last battle he did not expect the dragons to return.

"They are not coming to fight; they are coming to search for the Gem." Neras shouts.

"*They* still think it is hidden somewhere in the Gragin camp." Lonar shakes his head in frustration. "Even now, with everyone I've ever loved destroyed by those monsters they still return to bring further insult to my home." He tries to remind himself that none of this is their fault and their situation is itself dire but a lifetime of training to hate does not go away so easily.

Neras is still maneuvering himself into the crowded cave when he feels the intense heat behind him. It is nice until the tip of his tail starts to burn.

"AAAHHHH!" Neras screeches in pain pulling his tail the rest of the way into the cave. "Put it out, put it out!" He bellows in a panic when he sees that it is still aflame.

Slagradislaun pulls his cloak off from around his neck and tosses it onto the dragon's tail before dropping down on top of it himself. He feels the warmth of the flame on his stomach before it goes out. He jumps up, pulling his cloak off the injured Neras.

"Quick action." Neras compliments Slagradislaun. "Thanks for that."

Eclant kneels down to inspect the extent of his injuries.

"You're a little scorched. We'll have to keep it clean but you'll be fine." He declares.

"A little scorched? Are you kidding?" Neras questions looking for himself. "Wow, I thought I was on fire. That really hurts." He begins to whine until his eyes catch Larsynth watching him with pity. "Yeah, a little, no big deal." Neras backtracks.

The ground beneath them shakes as one of the large dragons lands outside the cave.

"We aren't done with you, Neras. You have betrayed us. Bring the last Gragin and all will be forgiven." Calls out the booming voice of Veralke.

"You don't understand," Neras begins to explain. "We've had it all wrong. The Gem isn't---" Before he can finish an echoing roar interrupts him.

"No more!" is the only answer he will get from his people.

They are never going to listen to what he has discovered. The stories are too deeply imbedded into who they are. If anyone could make them change their beliefs it certainly is not going to be a little runt who has never left the mountain caves before.

"I'm sorry, Neras but I think we're going to have to fight." Lonar concludes. "They're not going to let us out of this cave."

"I know. They'll let us starve in here if they don't burn us to death first." Neras sees they'll never give up on the Gem or returning to Narcor.

"Let me go out and catch him off guard from behind to get him away from the cave. Then the rest of you will be free to run." Slagradislaun offers.

"There's no back way out of the cave." Lonar explains. "How are you going to get behind him?"

Eclant smiles at the clever idea, "He's going to walk right out the front of the cave."

"You'll be charred alive!" Lonar exclaims.

"He'll be fine." Dervile assures him.

Slagradislaun steps forward to the cavern entrance. The dragon stands watch outside. Neras sees him leave the safety of the cave, his heart stops, convinced this will be certain death, but not sure how to stop him.

Slagradislaun stands in front of their jailor looking up at the incredible image. He carefully moves silently around Veralke who is still shouting threats at the cave entrance.

"How did he do that? Veralke is looking right at him but isn't reacting at all." Neras looks to the rest of the group in wonder.

Lonar is as confused by what he has witnessed, "How is that possible? Did the dragon actually let him pass?" He knows that cannot be right. Veralke did not register that he has seen Slagradislaun. "What is going on here?" He turns to Eclant for some answers.

"Yes, yes, I'm sure we'll have a conversation about what happened but for now you need to ready yourself. As soon as the dragon pulls away from the entrance we must charge out. You know better than any of us that one man alone cannot hope to fight and survive a dragon like that one." He cautions pointing to the huge beast outside. Slagradislaun is out of sight, now behind the dragon.

Lonar clutches his sword looking to Neras. He wants both permission and absolution. The small dragon turns his head, eyes filled with tears, away from Lonar. He nods in affirmation.

Twenty

SLAGRADISLAUN KNOWS HE WILL only have one chance to strike the dragon before the OverSight will no longer be his protection, and the enemy will be able to see that he is there. He has never fought a dragon before so he is not sure what the best plan of attack will be. The thick scales will not be easy to penetrate. As he contemplates what to do he sees the dragon's sides collapse as he inhales. Fearing that this is preparation for another, possibly disastrous, fiery strike into the cave Slagradislaun knows he does not have a second to spare. His assault has to be swift.

"Here goes," he whispers.

Without giving himself a chance to think twice about it, he sees a natural stairway leading straight up to a vulnerable spot on the dragon that will surely bring him down. Placing his right foot forward, he hunches his back before pushing off the ground with all of his power.

"One foot in front of the other, like a set of stairs, nothing but stairs." He tries to reassure himself, taking off.

Larsynth is ignoring the conversation going on behind her about how Slagradislaun is going to "sneak" past the dragon. She already knows the answer and is more concerned about his safety and watching for the ominous smoke. She sees the dragon pull in a deep drag, she knows what this means but there is no indication that his flame will hit his target. The air still smells the same, not pleasant, but not like death and for right now that is all she cares.

She watches the dragon's giant head lean down and forward to get a better look into the cave. Something is odd though. She does not know what she is seeing. It looks like something is growing out of the top of his head. It is not until the dragon lets out a spine chilling screech that she realizes its Slagradislaun and he is plunging both of his daggers into the dragon's right eye.

Neras jumps at the sound of the dragon, he had once respected, howling. His instinct is one of compassion and agony for his one-time family member. He wants to comfort him but has no doubt that the feeling is not mutual. When it comes to retrieving the Gem there is no sympathy to be had for a traitor. He is not sure what has happened to Veralke and cannot imagine what that tiny man can do from behind his enormous foe to cause such distress. He sees the others preparing to run out of the cave to assist Slagradislaun and fend off the enemy but he knows he cannot participate. He fears that his new companions will become untrusting of him for leaving them on their own against such a powerful adversary but his legs refuse to allow him to injure another dragon. His stomach churns at his cowardice.

Lonar is still trying to understand how Slagradislaun has managed to walk right passed a dragon. He is mentally preparing himself for yet another battle but he knows this one will be different. This time there is only one dragon and he has one of his own. It is small and cannot fly but a fire breathing machine none-the-less. His thoughts are interrupted by the most terrifying cry he has ever heard. He looks up in time to see Slagradislaun hanging from the handles of his daggers which appear to have been inserted into the eye of the dragon. He does not know how he got up there. The dragon's head is thrashing back and forth trying to shake free. Not one to miss an opportunity, Lonar lifts his sword straight out in front of his chest and flees his secure position. He hits the open air raising his sword high above his head. Lonar brings it crashing down on the bridge of the dragon's blood covered muzzle as it lands sideways on the ground still groaning from the pain inflicted on his eye.

Eclant is already outside the cave when Lonar comes running out rushing headlong at the fallen dragon like a man possessed. He screams incoherently as he plunges his sword into the bridge of the dragon's nose again and again. The poor creature cries out pitifully. Eclant has a certain amount of mercy for their beaten opponent. His whimpering cuts through Eclant like a shard of glass. Knowing the dragons' story, he thinks of this colossal creature as innocent and harmed by the King and all of those that came before him as Lonar's people have been. He cannot take it anymore; the unfortunate rival does not deserve this fate. Eclant's heart walks him toward Lonar, raising his hand in front of Lonar he whispers,

"Enough, let him go. This won't bring your people back. You know the truth and you know who is to blame for the deaths you've suffered and it is not he. Save your wrath for the one upon whose head it belongs, the King."

Dervile watches Eclant make his way to Lonar. He does not hear what is being said but he does not need to in order to understand the meaning of it. The fury that has overtaken Lonar is gradually fading as his strikes are less forceful. They no longer pierce the hide of the focus of his ire. Lonar's eyes gloss over as he is no longer in control of himself. Dervile knows the look of a man standing outside of himself and Lonar is not currently occupying his own body. He steps back and lets his sword slide down his hand onto the ground. He turns and walks back into the cave.

Neras can sense Lonar's rage when he comes through the entrance.

"Tell him to leave and never return. We will find the Gem and take it from the King. I'll do anything in my power to get your people back to their home. In the meantime, they better stay out of my way." Lonar never looks in Neras' direction.

He sits on a stone and loses himself staring into the flames of their campfire.

The rest of the group gathers back in the cave as their defeated attacker flies off back to the mountains. The silence is thunderous as they all avoid eye contact with Lonar. His raw emotion is palpable.

"What are the chances he'll return with help?" Dervile asks Neras shattering the quiet.

"They will return and there will be many more of them next time. We can't stay here." Lonar answers.

Neras shakes his head in agreement. Lonar lowers his head. He is coming back to his senses. He is ashamed of himself and how he has lost control.

"That can never happen again." He scolds. "If we are going to succeed, then I can't let my emotions take me over that way. I have to stay clear headed and keep my wits about me at all times. I won't let my people down a second time."

No one knows how to comfort him.

"It will take them awhile though," Neras explains to Dervile. "Nothing is ever done without the council's approval and that takes time."

Looking at out to the sky Larsynth concludes, "It's getting dark we should be safe until morning. If what you say is true, then I doubt they'll come back until day break."

"Yes, if we get an early start, we can stay here tonight." Neras confirms.

Little else is said as one by one, Dervile, Larsynth and Slagradislaun settle down for the night. Once the last of them is asleep Eclant knows it is time to let Lonar and Neras in on who their newest partners are and what are their stories. He begins with Dervile and Larsynth.

"I will summon these three to our aide first and foremost because they are all honorable people with fair minds, honest hearts and compassionate souls. As you have seen they also possess certain unusual abilities that can come in handy for our task at hand." Eclant pauses to make sure they are following him. "My old friend here and his daughter," he indicates with the wave of his hand in their direction. "They are from a long line of ancient people known as NecroSights."

"They see death coming, don't they?" Neras guesses thinking back to their fast reactions before the attack. As well as breaking down the meaning of the name, NecroSight.

"Correct, sir. No one knows how or why but it is the reason for their longevity. You see, Death, itself, is a coward. It fears the NecroSights because they have a sort of power where Death is concerned. As nothing else in the known world has any influence whatsoever in Death's tightly controlled realm, this is a concern. Because of Death's cravenness it will not come to a NecroSight unless compelled to do so by the will of another and even then Death remains hidden, NecroSights cannot use their ability to see their own or each other's time come. Only outright murder can kill a NecroSight. Neither disease nor famine is anything for them to fear. Thus, this is often a long lived race; if one can manage a quiet life with restricted dealing with the rest of the world that is. Since the beginning of the NecroSight line many, nearly all, have desired their abilities. Often they are hunted and enslaved by those who will use them to ensure their own safety. As the lives of most Kings and rulers are often cut short by those jealous of their authority, having a servant that can warn you of imminent personal attack is invaluable. Because of this, a large number of NecroSights believe that their gift is a curse. Therefore, it became the custom for NecroSights to ignore their visions of the fates of others and professing that it is not theirs to interfere with Death. Still others believe in the necessity of keeping the truth of who they are hidden, they want to help when able. For the past few hundred cycles the NecroSights have largely become a xenophobic, nomadic people purely for survival purposes. At heart most of them are social, gentle and kind." Eclant explains.

"Now our other friend is quite extraordinary as well. He is a Franeglian. Do you recall when they first entered camp?"

"Yes, at first I saw those two." Lonar recalls pointing to Dervile and Larsynth. "But not the other."

"Me too, I didn't notice him." Neras agrees.

"I didn't either because I didn't already know he'd be with them. But really a Franeglian traveling with NecroSights? Who will have ever expected to see that?"

"Not me!" Neras jokes having no idea what is so strange about it. Lonar smiles at the humor. Eclant shakes his head in agreement not catching the intended wit.

"So, why exactly didn't we see him?" Lonar presses. "Neither did the dragon." He adds.

"Right." Eclant realizes he needs to get back on track. "You see the Franeglian have something known as OverSight."

Eclant continues on through the next hour explaining to them all about Slagradislaun's people. Both Neras and Lonar can see how these three will be a tremendous help to them as they attempt to recover the Gem from the King.

"Why are they willing to put themselves in danger to help us?" Lonar wonders.

"Dervile has come in honor of the friendship that we share, that is to be certain." Eclant explains.

"And Slagradislaun?" Neras questions.

"He has his own reasons that have nothing to do with the three of us. He can be trusted."

"Now that we have them here, we had better come up with a plan." Lonar concludes.

"Yes, we won't be bothered again this evening but I can't say the same for tomorrow. We have no time to waste." Neras agrees.

"I've been thinking about that." Eclant grins. "I believe I have a rather ingenious idea."

The three bow their heads watching Eclant scratch through the dirt with a twig working out their next move.

Twenty-one

"WE CAN'T HAVE A DRAGON, albeit a small one, strolling around the town. Those people are already convinced that something awful may befall them at any moment." Eclant explains. "So, Neras, Larsynth and Dervile- you three will wait for us in the Ashford forest on the other side of the walled stronghold over there."

He points to the direction from which Slagradislaun, Larsynth and Dervile have come two days prior.

"We need as few people raising suspicion as possible," Lonar agrees. "The King has already met with me and I'm betting he'll do so again which will get the door open to the castle giving Slagradislaun a chance to slip in."

"More like, saunter right in under their noses." Larsynth clarifies smiling.

"I've been seen around these parts a few time in the past so I doubt I'll raise any eyebrows. I'll be along so that if something happens I can slide back and warn these two." Eclant says.

He is hesitant to express his concerns in that area as of yet.

"That all sounds reasonable. Excellent planning gentlemen." Dervile gives a half smile. The rest of the group begins packing up their things. Dervile pulls Eclant aside. He has been having the same concerns.

"I know that you can't slide back onto your own timeline but there is amble time for you to come to me again on our voyage here. Is that your plan? You can tell us exactly what we need to know."

"I have to admit that I've been wondering the same thing myself. I can't bring an object like the Gem through a slide with me but I believe that I can make this whole quest much easier on us. Other than your journey here though, there has not been much opportunity to get to any one of you when I wasn't already there. Patience is the order of the day; I believe that I will come to you all in the Ashford forest."

After talking it out with Dervile, Eclant has a plan. He commits to memory, for the future, this trip into Zulbarg. It is his chance to get to Dervile in Ashford forest. He, himself, will not be around which will avoid going back on his own timeline.

"We're all ready to head out." Slagradislaun calls to the men.

The group reaches the base of the hill outside the walls of Zulbarg and they separate into two groups. Larsynth, Dervile and Neras disappear into the forest to wait. Lonar approaches the gate to the town. The same man who had led him through the city to the castle during his last visit peers down at him from the guard's tower. Lonar waves trying to appear friendly. The man's head disappears. Lonar is getting nervous. Then, one of the giant doors opens enough for the head to reappear from behind it.

"Why are you here?" He questions Lonar.

"I have returned as bid by the King." Lonar lies, doubting that the King would have mentioned to his sentinels Lonar's likelihood of coming back either way.

"Fine." He steps aside for Lonar but eyes Eclant with uncertainty.

"He's with me." Lonar declares placing a hand on Eclant's elbow leading him through the gate. Unbeknownst to the guard,

Slagradislaun too marches into the town through the defensive structure.

This time as Lonar walks through the city, the sights and smells that so thrilled him on his last visit all fall flat and soured. His eyes do not leave the castle entrance as he marches, undistracted toward whatever ends this attempt will incur for him. The first guard leads the invaders forward, not a word is spoken to the man posted in front of the castle. He steps aside obediently allowing the men pass.

"I know where to go from here." Lonar asserts trying to shake their escort before coming face to face with the King, which he hopes to avoid.

"Until he tells me himself that you're free to wander the castle I will take you to the King." The guard retorts.

Lonar is prepared for the event that he may not be able to circumvent an audience with the King that is a chance they have all decided is worth taking. He does not think the King will find it unusual that a man who lost all of his family because he refused them aid may return to said King to have a few words. That is the part he is going to play, with no trouble.

The hallway is long and straight with a few small rooms shooting out from the sides of it. This allows Slagradislaun plenty of time to peer into each room for a quick look around and to inspect them for any possible hidden passages that may lead him to the Gem. He knows, of course, it will not be sitting on a side table like a common tchotchke. Slagradislaun manages to keep close to the others as they march on toward the King's chamber. His instincts as a descendant of a long line of thieves tell him that the valuable object is most likely to be kept close to the King himself if it really in the castle at all. Though they admittedly do not know for certain how the Gem works, all agree that it most likely needs to be near the people who it is controlling. This fact makes the castle the most probable location.

The guard stops, turning aside now, facing Lonar and Eclant, as well as Slagradislaun, though he does not know it, motioning for them to enter the room to his left. As they turn into the chamber Lonar stops short and is immobile at the scene before him. The King stands up from his seat at the large stone table covered with enough food to satisfy a man for a whole cycle. Looking directly at Lonar, the King flashes him a terrifying grin. He knew they were coming. He is expecting them. Lonar's body tenses with the awareness that their little theater is not going to work. His mind races, considering new options and throwing them away one by one as the flaws in each plan prove them useless. Eclant takes one step into the ambush, looking beyond the King to the other man at the table he bellows,

"Smaldi!"

Eclant disappears.

Twenty-two

ECLANT KNOWS IT IS A TRAP as soon as his eyes lock on that ever conniving Smaldi. He cannot let himself be captured until he brings this group together or all will be lost. He concentrates on his friend Dervile with all of his energy.

"I can't appear alarmed. I need to act like everything is normal and get them on their way to Zulbarg." He reminds himself.

However, sliding is disorientating and can usually leave you with a complete loss for when you are going and who you will be seeing. The slide makes his insides feel like they are being pulled out and twisted into a ball. His chest becomes heavy and breathing is a challenge. His landings are rarely without a certain amount of pain but the worst part is the short amount of time he has once he lands to do what he needs. The confusion can take too long to subside. He knows where and when he will find Dervile, Larsynth and Slagradislaun which gives him a better chance at landing in the right spot but it is anyone's guess what he will remember about why he has gone to them.

He is on the ground with his back side aching from disembarking the slide. As usual, his mind is a complete blank. Where is he? What is he doing here? He goes through his mental checklist which he performs after every slide; Look around and establish where you are. It appears to be the plains to the West. Next, do you see any one you know? How old are they?

Eclant spots a trio walking in front of him. The back of the tall man's head is familiar. Flowing white hair that closely matches his own;

"Ahhh," He sees it, the one unmistakable hint as to who he is looking at, the long white wooden walking staff.

"Dervile!" Eclant exclaims running toward him.

Dervile turns at the sound of his name and the familiar voice.

"Eclant, my old friend, you look well!" He smiles as his pal reaches him. The men embrace.

"As do you." Eclant replies. He turns, looking at the other party members. "Hello, Larsynth you look charmingly beautiful as ever."

"I'm sorry, sir, but I don't recall the last time we may have seen each other so I'm at a loss for your name." Eclant embraces her as some of the memory of what he is doing starts to return to him.

"I see Slag is here, but what about the others? Where are they?"

"Slag? As in the crud that gets stuck on the bottom of your boots?" Slagradislaun shoots him a look of both confusion and annoyance.

"You're thinking of sludge my dear boy," Eclant knows his time is running out. Why has he come here? He cannot get all the pieces together in his head.

"This is all wrong. Are you on your way to Zulbarg?" He cannot process why Lonar and Neras are not with them. Has he gone back too far?

"Zulbarg, why would we be going there?" Larsynth asks. All three of them look at him.

"Why? Because of the dragons!"

Eclant is trying not to become too exasperated with them but he can feel the pull and he knows he will be back in the slide soon.

"Lonar and Neras need your help. Scratch that, the entire kingdom needs your help. That damned King."

He can see Slagradislaun's impatience especially at the mention of Zulbarg.

"That's far away from where he's hoping to go." Eclant recalls to himself.

"I understand what you need from my friends, it's a wonderful and worthwhile cause and they'll help you I'm sure but that is going to take some time you understand. They have to find out where the mirror is and then you'll all have to go get it...*that* won't be easy with all the... It's a whole thing. I hope you understand why we need to focus on this first. The dragons are dying off and none of it is their fault..." Eclant spits it all out as fast as he can; hoping not to let this chance go by without making them understand as much as possible.

His head swirls and he feels the cold beginning to engulf him again. He knows this is it. He is not ready to go back to the castle yet so he closes his eyes tight and tries to concentrate.

"You must speak fast old man---" is all that Eclant hears from Dervile before he is sucked away into the slide.

The only thing he can think of is the look on Lonar's face when he walked into the King's chamber. He tries to focus and push it aside, but he can tell it is not working. A slide within a slide is particularly difficult to pull off and takes a great deal of skill and practice. He decides that it is best not to fight it. Eclant puts all of his focus on Lonar.

Eclant's landing feels odd to him, bumpy and loud. He looks around at the emptiness. He knows this cannot be right, there is not another person here. He cannot slide to a time and place without someone else being there. The ground beneath him is jostling his body about. He peers down, realizing he has landed directly on top of Lonar,

"Oh, my word that is dreadfully precise now isn't it? I do apologize. That must have been an extraordinary show of concentration on my part won't you say?"

Eclant labors to get up off of the man but his head is swimming and he has no control of his own extremities.

"Just stop and let me."

"Yes, a much better plan I'd say." Eclant agrees.

He stops moving to allow Lonar to take control of the situation. He stares up at the sky and is surprised to realize that it is night. He can figure out *where* he is. He sees that they are on the topmost part of the castle.

"Why would Lonar be up here?"

He cannot figure out when in their relationship he has managed to land. He is not sure what message to give.

"I meant for you to hold still a minute not for the rest of eternity."

Eclant feels his whole body lifting off the ground.

"This is it," he thinks. "I am being pulled back through. I've failed."

Eclant tries to concentrate as hard as he can on Neras. He hopes he will at least be able to reach him. One more slide is unlikely but he has to try. He waits for the unmistakable feeling of the slide to begin. Instead, he is being lowered to the ground. He opens his eyes to see that he is not sliding at all. Lonar has picked him up and is setting him upright in place. He is overcome with joy. Hope is not lost; he has not failed!

"I suppose that is silly of me. I don't really have degrees of motion it is usually all or nothing with me you know." Eclant tries to explain.

"As a matter of fact, I don't know."

Eclant feels a tension that he does not expect.

"Right, yes, of course, you won't." He backs off a bit.

"So, you okay then?" Lonar is preoccupied by something but Eclant cannot make out what it might be since he still does not know when he is.

"Yes, fine, sure." He does a quick inventory of himself to discover all is well.

Lonar turns to walk away. Eclant knows the conversation is over as far as he is concerned. Trying to think fast, he calls out after him.

"No, no I'm not. I'm... broken. My left ankle." He lies not aware that he picked up the wrong foot in his deceitful attempt to keep Lonar there.

"Well, you seem to be standing on it fine."

Catching his mistake, Eclant switches feet. The pull is coming back. Trying not to panic he knows he does not have any more time for these games.

"No, you see, what I mean is I have important information for you. It's about the King and the dragons. You see---"

The strength of the slide increasing.

"It can't be time;" he thinks to himself.

"Oh no, not already. Yes, of course, well there is me landing on you and the falling and all that... I guess it did take some time but really..."

He does not grasp that he has been talking out loud until the slide knocks the wind out of him with his final words. Three slides at once is incredibly dangerous but he is determined to at least try it. He thinks of Neras, he pictures him in the forest hopeful that he can warn him, Dervile and Larsynth about the trap. They cannot save him but at least they would know what has happened.

This time, Eclant's landing is particularly harsh. His head is being crushed by an invisible force. His whole body feels broken. Whatever he has landed on is loud and hot. His legs are burning.

"AAAGGGG!" Not again! Will you kindly please?" Eclant calls out, afraid he is going to burn to death before he can manage to get his bearings.

"Who are you? What are you doing?" Neras shouts.

Eclant recognizes the voice but still is not able to piece together what is happening. He is relieved to see Lonar's head pop out from around the bushes and chuckle.

"Yes, sorry. I seem to be more focused than ever today." He cannot comprehend how he has managed to safely perform three slides.

"Eclant here. As you no doubt have guessed I am a Darist."

Eclant is hoping to move past the introductions as quickly as possible this time.

"No doubt," Eclant cannot tell if Neras means what he says or not.

"So, this is our first meeting, Neras?"

"Yes, I...Wait, how do you know my name?"

"He does that." He can now see all of Lonar as he comes out from what must have been a hiding spot.

"Ah, my friend, how are you?" Eclant bows happy to see Lonar.

"Just glad I wasn't the one you landed on this time."

I will think." Eclant smirks relieved that he is doing something in the right order.

"You remember, the last time when you landed on me?" Lonar cannot read his reaction.

"Yes, yes." Eclant says rubbing is leg smiling. "No bother, we have more important things to discuss and little time. Soon, Dervile, Slag and Larsynth will be here, I do hope. I can give you the part of the story that neither of you has, you must piece the rest yourselves. I won't have time."

"What?" Neras asks but Eclant does not have time to stop and explain any more than he has to. These two must work things out for themselves. He will be pulled back through the slide before long.

"Now, you both must listen closely and don't interrupt me. The ancient King of Zulbarg thought the Gragin were too easily able to conquer his kingdom. There were always few but you are a powerful clan. At least you were, I'm sorry friend." He knows what he is saying has to be painful for Lonar but there's no have time to mince words for anyone's sake. It is hard to see the pain in Lonar's eyes at the mention of his lost ones. Eclant knows if he is to carry on he cannot be side tracked by guilt. He looks toward the ground in attempts to keep his train of thought. "Therefore, he brought the dragons here to take care of the threat. Sharsin never touched the Gem of C'Vard." He knows he has to make that part absolutely clear to the both of them.

He sees their confusion but he still has to tell them the most important detail and he is already feeling the pull.

"The Gem instills fear in people. It makes them believe that everything around them can turn into something evil or harmful, even the most benign thing like, water." It is the best analogy he can come up with at the time looking at the pond. "It can make them think that it is poison. It is powerful and dangerous but it is not what holds your people here." He has to make sure Neras understands that point. "My time nearly is up. Tell each other your story. Don't trust the King and talk---"

He hopes they cannot hear his screams as the slide takes him again. He does not want to scare his friends but something is wrong. His lungs are burning; this is not from the slide as usual. This is different. He is drowning.

Twenty-three

ECLANT TRIES NOT TO GASP for breath knowing that it will make him swallow more water, but it is a difficult instinct to fight. He does not think he can battle his body's inclination to struggle for air much longer. He feels the water rushing over him as he is pulled out and into a new slide.

"The pond, I was thinking about the pond, that's how I ended up here."

Four slides are not possible. He has completed three with various degrees of success but a fourth throws everything out of whack. He cannot imagine where he will land next or if he will survive it at all. The nature of the slide is to go to one place in time and then be boomeranged back to where you were. Two slides have been accomplished but the farther into the multiples of slides you try to go the more force the yo-yoing back to your starting point. It is like stretching a rubber band farther and farther before letting go. He is on the letting go end of the slide and it has been stretched as far as anyone has ever done. The key is for Eclant to clear his mind and allow the slide to take him back. He cannot silence his brain. The fear and desperation to complete his task are ever present. Each thought during the slide is taking him to a new destination and pulls the rubber band more and more.

Eclant is dumped out of the slide on to a stone path. His senses take longer than usual to come to him. He coughs up a bit of water. He is looking around trying to pinpoint his location. He is in a town that much is clear. It is crowded and there are people all around him. He looks in front of him and sees the back of someone he knows again. This isn't Dervile, that much he can muster. He cannot get his mind to retrieve who exactly it is but he knows this is someone familiar to him. He tries to open his mouth to cry out but no sound comes as the identity still escapes him. The best he can force his body to do is grab the back of the man's tunic.

"Eclant. I am Eclant." Is all he can manage as every part of his being aches and burns.

He twists his head and reaches for his hair, beginning to ring it out. This man does not show any indication of recognizing who he is. Eclant identifies the young man but as he opens his mouth to say his name, before anything can come out, he feels himself crash to the ground again. A child screeches as he runs by carelessly knocking him over. With nothing more than a glance back the kid takes off joyfully skipping away. Again, Eclant begins to fumble his way trying to get back on his feet. Lonar reaches down, grabbing Eclant by the wrist and with one tug pulls the man back into place.

"Thank you." Eclant says brushing himself off.

"Watch out for the little ones," Lonar smiles at Eclant warming him with good will, but as of yet, has no idea who this strange man is or how important he will become in his life.

"Crazy old fool, pay him no mind. We're almost there." Eclant hears the guard command, as the two hurry off on their way.

Eclant is motionless, trying to place when he has landed. He knows this must be the first time Lonar has ever met him but his brain is failing him. He attempts to work out when and why Lonar would be in Zulbarg. As the answer begins to come to him, the familiar tug of the slide beckons to him again. This time he closes his eyes and thinks of nothing but the emptiness in front of him. His insides twist and his chest pushes down on him. He can sense that something is wrong with the slide. He is going far too fast. Time moves at a particular pace and this is not right. The rubber band is snapping and there is no telling what it is going to do. Eclant prepares himself for the worst.

The skin on his legs is being torn as the slide is dropping him in his beginning place. His back and arms burn. The force of being snapped back to where he was before his first slide is ripping him apart. He tries to scream but there is no air in his lungs to do so. When he lands, the pain is excruciating. He opens his eyes in time to see Smaldi reach for his neck before he passes out from his misery.

Eclant can hear yelling that sounds like it is coming from Lonar. He cannot make out what is being said. He opens his eyes to see Smaldi standing over him smirking with pleasure at the sight of this once great man tattered and beaten. The bile in Eclant's stomach chokes him at the sight of the traitor. He turns his focus to the wellbeing of Lonar and Slagradislaun. He hears Lonar's screams. He rolls his neck, pointing his head in the direction of the sound to see Lonar with his broad sword under the chin of the King. He is demanding that he be told what has been put on Eclant's neck. Eclant tries to reach his hand up to his throat to touch the cold metal object strangling him but he does not need to, he knows what it is. He lets his head drop back to where Smaldi is whispering threats of torture in his ear. He cannot make out the words but the intention is clear.

Eclant is in a daze. He is trying to take in as much of the scene as he can but is unable to process it. His mind is too foggy with pain and confusion. Eclant blinks, he cannot make sense of what he is seeing now. From behind Smaldi's head a glint appears, blinding Eclant. He squints at the brightness. He thinks he sees Slagradislaun's face. It lifts up from behind Smaldi's right shoulder as if he is watching a strange growth appear out of nowhere. Eclant sees a quick movement across Smaldi's torso followed by a bib of blood forming down the front of his lifeless body. Eclant cringes watching Smaldi's face coming closer to his own, eyes wide open, still in triumph. Slagradislaun grabs the corpse by the shoulders and tosses it aside preventing it from landing on top of him. Eclant is thankful. Slagradislaun shouts to Lonar,

"Forget him, grab Eclant and let's get out of here!" Eclant feels himself floating before blacking out once again.

Twenty-four

WANDERING AROUND ASHFORD FOREST, Larsynth is taking a little time to herself. The circumstances of what has happened over the past few days are overwhelming. This is the first chance she has had to enjoy a little silence and just breathe. She is trying not to think about what might be happening in the castle, it should be an easy enough chore but, there are no guarantees. Unsure of what to expect when the three men return, she is imagining all the possible outcomes. She is running over each scenario laying out the most appropriate next step. This has always been a soothing process for her. Dervile worries that this is not healthy for a young girl, he only sees the negativity in it. Yet, for Larsynth, it is her way to feel prepared. After losing her mother so unexpectedly Larsynth has become obsessive about having everything in order. In her mind, order means control. She never felt so powerless as she did when her mom died and she never wants to feel like that again. The aimlessness and disorientation of that loss is ever present in her. But, she can do her best to not allow it to take her over again, like it had during her sorrow.

She hears someone coming toward her. The rustle of the leaves and breaking of the twigs on the ground indicate that whoever it is, they are in a hurry. Larsynth turns her head to call out to her father and Neras as Slagradislaun breaks through the foliage.

"Eclant... he's hurt... maybe dead." He manages, panting from the long run. "Get your dad and Neras. We have to help Lonar. The King's men are behind us." Slagradislaun is bent over trying to catch his breath.

Larsynth, knows she cannot shout or they will be discovered. She sprints through the woods hoping that Slagradislaun is wrong about Eclant being dead. Reaching the makeshift campsite where her father and Neras are waiting, Larsynth anxiously begins screaming out to them.

"Eclant's dead!" She regains control of herself and lowers her voice. "At least he's hurt. I don't know how bad. The guards are chasing Lonar and Slagradislaun. We have to help them. NOW!"

Dervile and Neras jump up from their seats against two trees. She bawls out the final words, her heart racing in her chest. She is feeling out of control again. This is when the panic takes over. Closing her eyes, she cannot calm her initial nervousness. She tries to become the master of her emotions again. Slagradislaun reaches the camp.

"This way." He is motioning, "Lonar has Eclant and some of the guards chased us out of the town."

They all take off, following Slagradislaun. Dervile is lively for someone of his advanced age. Larsynth is faster than her father but is lagging behind him keeping an eye on Neras. The dragon lacks the agility of the rest of the group and lumbers on as best as he can.

"What about Eclant? What happened?" Dervile is demanding more answers as they run.

"I don't know. He popped out, when he came back he was ripped up and bleeding."

The whooshing sound of an arrow comes between the two of them, interrupting their conversation and causing them to take cover. Neras notices the men in front of him are no longer running. He is not sure what is happening or why they have both stopped and disappeared off in another direction. Not seeing the archer in his way; Neras is scanning the area where his friends have dipped behind the trees when he loses his balance. He is trying, unsuccessfully, to stop himself. He falls forward, letting out a squeal. He attempts to be as quiet as possible so as to not call attention to himself.

Neras lays on his stomach on the ground feeling a most uncomfortable pinching sensation underneath him. A perplexed expression crosses his face as he considers the sound he has heard.

"Wait, that wasn't me. I don't make that sound."

A prick in his gut causes Neras to start rolling back and forth, trying to get all the way to one side or the other to allow him use his short front arms to propel himself off of the ground.

"Hold on, let us help." Dervile is standing next to the fallen dragon.

He and Slagradislaun are each grabbing an arm, pulling Neras backward and onto his feet again.

"Oh!" Larsynth is suppressing a chortle, reaching the area where the rest of them are loitering.

Dervile tries, too, to resist a giggle of his own.

"The indignity." Neras is blushing.

"Ah! Good work!" Slagradislaun punches Neras in the shoulder.

Seeing what everyone is talking about Neras grins.

"Got him good, didn't I?" Pretending that killing the archer was his intention all along.

"I think it was the rolling back and forth over his crushed body that did the trick." Slagradislaun is roaring with laughter as his words are barely able to be understood.

Emerging through the brush Lonar is exhausted and out of breath.

"There are two behind me" he is yelling as his legs give out from underneath him, with Eclant in his arms, he collapses to the ground.

"I'm on it!" Slagradislaun calls back as he takes off.

"I better go keep an eye on him." Larsynth bounds into the thicket without giving her father a chance to object.

The pair does not have far to go before catching up with the men the King has sent after them.

"Three men? That's almost insulting." Slagradislaun smirks. Neras has already taken out one that leaves Slagradislaun face to face with these two. Both men are huge and carry large battle axes. This is fine for Slagradislaun; big means slow and he is fast. The first man lifts his axe up over his head. Bending his elbows, he drops his weapon down behind his back preparing for the hard crash forward. This is not effective when fighting someone much more agile than yourself. The axe does not make its way back over the man's head before he has both of Slagradislaun's daggers protruding from his chest. Larsynth gasps as she witnesses the black smoke begin to appear for a second time, unsure which of the two remaining will be the next victim.

Twenty-five

DROPPING TO THE GROUND, Slagradislaun manages to avoid the slicing of his opponent's blade. The wind comes off of it as it passes over his head. He knows this was a close call. On all fours, he looks over to his enemy, as expected, his powerful swing of the axe caused him to lift up off of his right leg. His lack of balance can prove to be a fatal error. Slagradislaun pushes his whole body upward, twisting it as he does, launching both legs sideways and into the legs of his attacker, dropping him to the ground. As the King's man comes plummeting down he loses his hold of the hefty axe, sending it flying backward. It knocks the bow that Larsynth is trying to ready out of her hands. She knows what is coming but doubts if she is prepared for it. The guard's weapon bounces off of a nearby tree and rests on the ground near her bow. She has to act. The man is back up and coming at Slagradislaun. She reaches into her boot and grabs the dirk she got off the man at the market. She feels her feet moving underneath her. She is not sure that a decision has been made until she finds herself standing over the man with the blade raised high above her head. She looks into his eyes as, without her permission, her arms start driving the small blade into his chest over and over again until she no longer has the strength to keep going. Never before has she felt so much hatred. The anger and rage are in charge. She is out of control. Slagradislaun reaches out, touching her hands, exhausted, she drops the weapon onto the ground. She calms herself. She may not regret having to kill the man but she will regret watching the reality of his death come true in his eyes as she does so. A single tear falls from her right eye as she looks into his Slagradislaun's face. She understands now why he is so adamant about his people losing their power to kill without prejudice. What a silly little girl she has been; thrilled with the prospect of an adventure. If this is what adventure is all about she would thankfully go back to a dull life.

"Come on, more will be coming after a while. We need to see about Eclant." Slagradislaun whispers as he pulls his bloody daggers from the man he has killed and wipes them clean in the grass.

"Does the blood ever come off?" She asks in a haze, watching him.

"Not really." He answers, sheathing them again.

The two walk in silence until they see Neras' bold blue scales standing out from all of the green and brown of the forest like a beacon calling them back to their circle of comfort. As she stands next to her father she cannot fight the need to have his arms around her. She would give anything for him to tickle her feet, waking her up from this nightmare. She wants to reach for him, but he is seeing to Eclant's wounds and this is no time for her to act like a child. She has to be strong, an adult. Crossing this milestone is a one-way trip.

Neras picks up Eclant. "He is in no condition to walk and we won't be safe staying here."

"There are a few inns around but they will be the first places to be searched." Dervile puzzles.

144

"I think it is best for now to get as far away from Zulbarg as we can. The paranoid King won't send his men too far from home." Lonar points out.

They carry on west until they have been walking for most of the day. Confident this is as far as they need to be, Dervile has them make camp while he checks on Eclant's wounds. He was able to find most of the roots and leaves he needs to treat them before they left the forest. He was sure to bring along a good supply to keep his care going. Eclant sleeps through the night and does not open his eyes again until midday.

"I remember little from yesterday. Where are we?" He asks looking around at the unfamiliar surroundings.

"Far west of the city. Safe." Dervile answers. "You gave me an awful turn, old man. I've heard that a slide can go badly but I never expected this." He says, indicating Eclant's wounds.

"I slide four or five times, I can't recall." Eclant announces.

"Well, how about you don't try that again." Dervile is happy to see his mood is upbeat.

"Agreed…" A memory is coming back to him.

"Smaldi!" Eclant jumps forward clutching his neck in a panic.

Seeing his reaction Slagradislaun squats down next to him.

"I'm sorry if that was a friend." He apologizes. "But it surely looked like he meant you harm after he put that thing around your neck."

"I assure you, that devil is no friend to me or any other Darist." Eclant comforts him.

"Smaldi?" Dervile asks, he has heard tales but never believed they are actually true. "I thought he was a Darist too."

"He can slide but he is no Darist!" Eclant corrects.

Not wanting to argue with his friend, Dervile let his side of the conversation drop.

"He's done this to me!" Eclant cries out tugging at the metal noose around his neck.

"What is that?" Dervile leans forward examining the peculiar object.

"A Time Lock" Eclant despairs.

"Oh, come now." Dervile is incredulous. "It can't be. Where would Smaldi possibly manage something like that? They were rare to begin with but I don't think there have been any working Time Locks around for more than a thousand cycles. Not since before my own conception. Many people don't believe those stories were actually true."

"I assure you, they are all too real. The problem is that a lot of fantasy has been mixed in with the reality. I must admit that I don't know enough to be able to distinguish the two." Eclant confesses.

"I don't know how to be of help to you my dear friend." Dervile asks.

"I fear we have no choice but to go north into the mountains of Parthectra." Eclant is firm.

"Do you think the Oracle is still there after all of these cycles?" Dervile is not sure what to think.

"I can't say, but for all of our sakes, I sure hope he is. I know the journey will be a difficult one but I fear more what will become of our quest without the Oracle's help removing the Time Lock."

"It's going to be a long trip all the way to the top of the mountain where the Oracle is said to reside. How are we going to get Eclant up there in his condition?" Lonar inquires in a hushed voice.

"Should we wait until he heals up enough to make it?" Slagradislaun offers.

Dervile leans into the circle also keeping his voice down so as to not wake the sleeping Eclant.

"I understand your thought but I fear this situation is too dire. Besides, we'd have as long of a journey to find ourselves safe refuge from the King's men."

"I can carry him the rest of the way. It slows us down a bit but I think it's our best option considering the circumstances." Neras declares.

"That will make for a bumpy and uncomfortable ride for poor Eclant." Larsynth eyes the old man with sorrow. "These first two days of traveling are already taking its toll on him. This is the time he needs to be healing."

"I can give him some more Greptis root for the pain and enough Wofurt to keep him asleep, that should help but we need to keep him off of his back. Those wounds are deep." Dervile concludes.

"I have an idea, something similar to a contraption I read about once."

Neras reaches for a long twig off of the nearest tree. Snapping it in thirds he puts two sticks side by side on a tall stump in the center of where the group is standing. He then snaps the remaining twig into thirds again.

"We tie the smaller pieces across these two, at the top, middle and bottom." He arranges his collection.

"Now, we need to get a large piece of cloth, like a blanket and wrap it around two larger branches..."

Larsynth hands him her handkerchief to use as a prop.

"Thanks. Now we wrap it and tie it in the back. Like this." He manipulates the cloth around the outsides of the larger limbs.

"I can't tie it now, not without the centerpieces being secured in place but you see the idea." Neras hopes.

"My, that's genius!" Dervile grins for the first time in days.

"I think if we put rope on the handles I'll be able to put it around my waist and bring him along that way. It'll still be uncomfortable and mighty bumpy-"

"But we can keep him off of his back!" Dervile is thrilled with this idea.

Everyone else nods in agreement that this is the best choice available to them to make the trek as easy on Eclant as possible.

Eclant cannot make out everything that is being said but he knows they are talking about him. His wounds are painful but not life-threatening. He agonizes over becoming a burden to those he had intended to help. He is a fool for being tricked but so loathsome a character as Smaldi. They have a long history of hatred between them. He cannot grasp how the King and Smaldi managed to come together for the deed. He replays the events in the chamber in his head as best as he can; trying to make sense of it. It happened too fast. He stifles a smile at the thought that Smaldi is dead. This does bring him solace but does not fix the problem. He feels the weight of the metallic snare hanging around his neck. His only hope now is the Oracle.

Twenty-six

SLAGRADISLAUN POKES AT THE FIRE. The embers give off little more than a dim glow. He can feel the heat radiating off Larsynth so strongly it is as though the flames are still raging. They have been traveling into the mountains of Parthectra for nearly a week. Dervile believes that they are a little more than a couple more weeks away. Eclant is on the mend from his ordeal at the castle but is weak. Thinking back on it now, it is another lifetime as their new circumstances have sent them so far off their original path. Once he becomes healthy enough, Eclant will try to slide. It has become evident that the man who did this to him, is working either for, or, with the King. Complicating things more, the King knows what they are up to. No one is certain how much of their plan is clear to the tyrant. He at least knows that Eclant is working with Lonar and a Franeglian. The hope is that he does not know about Neras or what it is they were doing in the castle. It could have appeared to him that Lonar was seeking revenge for the lack of assistance from Zulbarg that caused the rest of his family to perish. They did not manage to get near the Gem. They agree that in light of how important and useful Eclant's sliding can be to them, they have to find out what they can about removing the Time Lock from his neck. Dervile has heard a great deal about the Oracle in the mountains. He trusts that the Oracle may also offer some additional help to them. There is a lot they do not know about the Gem. Most importantly, as Slagradislaun pointed out, they do not know how to destroy it.

Dervile and Eclant both agree that a magical item like that is not going to be able to be demolished with mere brute force, it is going to require counter magic. That is something none of them knows anything about.

For now, Slagradislaun is focused on being grateful for this beautiful night. Larsynth is sitting beside him enjoying the flicker of the flames. She has become the first real friend he has ever had. The thought makes Slagradislaun lean in toward Larsynth. He takes in her scent. She can feel him moving next to her. She lets her leg inch closer in his direction waiting for the right moment to relax it against him. The others are almost asleep. This is the part of the day that the two of them relish.

By the time Eclant is snoring, they know they are safe to step into the world where only they exist. The conversation starts off by discussing the events of the day and considering what tomorrow might bring. But, as it always does, it moves into a deeper sharing of their real hopes and dreams. Larsynth opens up to Slagradislaun about her father and how much she loves him. She talks about how frightened she is for his wellbeing. He wants to reach for her and reassure her that he will do everything in his power to keep her beloved father safe. He, too, has developed a great affection for Dervile. Slagradislaun tells her how he was raised to be a merciless fighter and that he always knew he could not live the typical life of a Franeglian. He is an outcast. She longs to make him see that he is the most special thing that has ever come into her life. They talk like this for hours, as they do every night under the stars. Larsynth once told him that all the best conversations of her life happen after midnight. He told her that all the best conversations of his life happen with her.

Off in the distance, they hear what sounds like a cracking of a twig. Slagradislaun and Larsynth jump to attention. They both stand still listening. A second crack is heard; they are off in its direction. Larsynth is agile and has a certain amount of stealth on her side but Slagradislaun is downright invisible. As they get beyond the camp and into the clearing they can now see the culprit. It is a Swatalin boar. They are fierce but also tasty and can feed the group for two days. Slagradislaun and Larsynth know it will have to be theirs. Swatalin boars are fast and dangerous; they have two large tusks which they wield like swords. Luckily, they are also stupid.

Slagradislaun catches its attention by tossing a pebble at it, making him now visible to the prey. He coaxes it the right giving Larsynth the opportunity to flank it on the left. The boar begins to charge Slagradislaun. It whips its head around turning the enormous tusks into two huge battering rams. Slagradislaun takes a step to the left as Larsynth lands a blow to the back of the boar with her arrow, slowing him down. She reaches out, grabbing the arrow like a handle she pushes down on it with all of her strength. It tears the skin straight down its back. The boar goes into a fury. It starts to run around the clearing with its blood flying everywhere. It turns the peaceful green landscape into a blood stained battle zone. Slagradislaun can see that it is heading back toward Larsynth but knows she is swift enough to dodge it. She is not moving; instead, she is looking at a different part of the field, smiling.

"What is she doing?" Slagradislaun wonders. He remembers, she is a NecroSight, she must be seeing the boar die. She does not notice the living version of the boar coming right at her.

Slagradislaun rushes to her side, grabbing her and pulling her back out of its path. The boar darts by. It begins to slow down and falls over dead in the same spot Larsynth has been watching. Larsynth gives out a cheerful noise and looks up at Slagradislaun.

Her brown eyes soften his soul and he wants to wrap her up in his arms. He holds her in his grasp looking down at her. Larsynth stares back into his face. He can feel her silky hair falling between his fingers. She leans forward and pecks his cheek then presses the side of her face against his.

"Come, let's take our prey back to the fire and prepare it. I want to know your thoughts on the afterlife." Larsynth says. Slagradislaun retrieves the boar, heartbroken.

Twenty-seven

"**I**T'S BEEN FOUR DAYS SINCE we finished that boar," Dervile is concerned, "We are weak from hunger and Eclant needs nutrition to heal."

He looks to his friend still asleep on the cot they made for him before heading off on this journey. The base of the Parthectra Mountains is still a way off and they are already in dire trouble. Larsynth and Eclant are so malnourished that they cannot travel anymore and Dervile and Slagradislaun are not far behind.

"This whole place is barren. There's nothing here." Lonar points out with frustration. The sturdy nature of his people has allowed for him to keep his strength up longer than the others.

"If we don't find food soon, none of us will make it much longer." Slagradislaun agrees, too weak to lift his head, joining the conversation.

Neras has not been having as much trouble dealing with the deserts of Zonthia as the warm, dry atmosphere is perfect for dragons. However, at this point, he too is suffering the effects of going without food. He listens as the morning discussion comes to an end and the others drift off to sleep again. "Neras, you awake?"

He hears Lonar whispering his name.

"Yeah?"

"We have to do something. You and I are the only ones with enough energy left to find food or help. Do you see that hill in the distance there?" Lonar points to the north.

"Do you think there's something over there other than more sand?" Neras hopes.

"I heard Dervile and Eclant saying they thought we'd be coming to the edge of Zonthia any day now. It is up to us to go on as far as we can to get the others help or we'll all die here."

"I think you're right. It has to be us." Neras agrees.

"And it has to be now. Do you think you can?" Lonar asks.

Neras struggles to lift himself off of the ground and creeps over to Lonar who is also fighting to find the strength to stand. He reaches his claw out, allowing Lonar to grab it. Neras pulls him the rest of the way up. They both trudge through the wasteland toward the large hill of sand. Neither is sure how they will manage to make it over the hill. They do not know what is on the other side or if they will be able to save their friends but it is the one chance they have.

As the day wears on, the heat of the sun zaps what little energy the duo has left. With each step, the sand pulls their feet under and does its best to keep them trapped in that spot. Before sunset they reach the base of the mound.

"I don't think I can make it, not uphill." Lonar chokes.

His skin is throbbing red from the sun beating down on him all day. He is so dry from dehydration that his tongue is swollen making it difficult to breath and speak. The skin around his lips is chapped and flaking off. His body gives way and he falls to the ground sinking a bit into the sand. He closes his eyes.

Neras looks back at his friend. He stares at his chest to make sure Lonar is still breathing. He knows there is not much time left. Thankfully, the retreating of the sun will give him some relief. Knowing that it is all down to him, Neras is being crushed by the weight of the lives resting on his shoulders. He must make it over this hill. More than that, there has to be something on the other side besides more sand, or they are all doomed. He eyes the peak of his nemesis vowing to himself that he will conquer it. Step by step, he is more acutely aware than before the sheer heft of his body as it sinks and stumbles its way ever higher.

"Almost there. I can nearly reach out and touch it." Neras calls back to Lonar. He does not know if his friend is still conscious but he hopes his encouraging words will help Lonar hold on. He takes a slow blink as his neck begins to fail to holdup his head. It bounces around as he tries to regain control. He forces himself to continue climbing as the sand gives way under him, sliding back down the hill. He cannot walk and keep his eyes open any more, there is not enough left in him to do both. He reaches the summit, a wave of relief rushes over him. He collapses. Somehow, his body is still moving. He cannot make his head stop swirling around and he feels the sand shifting underneath him from the force of his body flopping down on it. There is a new sensation. He is sweating. A lot. He knows that dragons do not sweat, he cannot make sense of what is happening. Now, he is drowning in the sweat. Or is the sand enveloping him and pulling him down to his death?

Neras opens his mouth to call for help. When he does, his tongue comes alive.

"Water!"

He cannot believe it. He opens his eyes still lapping at the cool refreshing lifeline. He finds himself sitting, waist deep in a small pond. He blinks a few times trying to focus his eyes. Looking around he realizes that he was not dizzy before, he had actually rolled down the other side of the hill and landed in a fish pool. He splashes around in it, drinking as fast as his throat will allow and cleaning the sand off of his scales. He is about to laugh out loud when he spies a large cabin nearby surrounded by many smaller ones in a semi-circle on the other side of the pond. He stops, lowering himself into the water so that only his head is visible. Scanning the area, he takes inventory of the scene. The main large cabin is in the middle facing the pond. Making a horseshoe, the smaller cabins are situated on either side of the longone, ten in all. While the large cabin looks quite nice and in good repair the others could best be described as hovels. They have holes in the roofs and the wood along the bottoms is rotted away allowing small creatures an easy entrance. They are all locked tight with chains.

Beyond the cabins are small plots of farmed land and fruit trees. There are also a few small barns with what he can smell as goats, lambs and pigs. Something about this place is not right to Neras but he cannot decide what it is. His thoughts focus on the food that he can see. He wades to the far right side of the pond, out of view of any cabin windows. He stops to fill up the four canteens he has been carrying with him and creeps toward the feast waiting for him.

Around the back of the first cabin, Neras hunches over as much as he can. He takes long, slow strides as he creeps around the buildings toward the fields. On the rear side of the big cabin there is a row of large baskets. He contemplates if it is worth the risk. Considering he has four more people he needs to nourish, he does not see any other way to get enough food back to them without the baskets. He slinks between the barns until he reaches the containers. He grabs one, turning to the banquet. He pulls different fruits from the trees tossing some into the basket and others directly into his own mouth. He knows their natural juices will help to hydrate the party as he can already feel himself coming back to life. He glances through the fields but is not able to identify what anything is so he decides to skip it and risk a much better prize, meat. He peeks in each barn. He knows enough about hunting to determine that his best option of pulling this off is to find one animal away from the others. It will reduce the chances of the alarm being raised and foiling his plot. Unfortunately, each stable is small containing only a half a dozen of each livestock which are all housed together. If he gets caught, all of his friends could die. He decides that it is not worth it.

He has enough to at least get everyone back on their feet so that they can come here and present themselves as travelers asking for hospitality. There is no time to waste. He takes in his surroundings and plans his best route back to the hill. He can see that from where he is, walking directly behind the small cabins on his left will take him around to the pond directly at the base of the hill. He ducks behind the nearest hut and begins to creep along. He stops when he hears the sound of chains moving. The noise ceases. He is free to continue.

He hears it again, halting, he looks around but still sees nothing that could be making the sound.

"Jokon, stop moving about, we're trying to sleep." A disembodied voice commands.

"Sorry." A smaller one apologizes.

Neras is alarmed to discover that the exchange is coming from inside the small cabin. Looking a few steps ahead of himself he can see where a rotten part of the cottage has disintegrated. He crawls over to it, peering in.

He is stunned by what he witnesses inside. Straw covers a dirt floor, laying on the chaff are five young boys, between the ages of six and thirteen. Each is on his back with his ankles chained to the wall. Neras stifles a gasp. He cannot figure out what he is seeing. He moves to the next cabin and finds a place to examine its contents. He finds the same scene. It repeats itself with the next hut and again in the next. He is shaken by what he has observes. However, he must first take care of his friends.

He bounds up the hill this time and finds Lonar motionless at the bottom. Neras pulls his body out from the intruding sand. He pushes his head back, opening his mouth and drizzles in the life reviving water. Lonar opens his eyes. Surprised to see a dragon looking down at him he jumps with a start.

"It's just me." Neras reminds him.

Coming to his senses, Lonar looks around, "You made it?"

"Yes, and you aren't going to believe what I found. First things first, let's get this back to camp." He holds up his basket of fruit. Lonar's eyes widen at the sight.

Twenty-eight

"CHILDREN?" LARSYNTH IS APPALLED by what she is hearing from Neras.

"Definitely, children." He reassures everyone.

"We have to go there and find out what's going on," Eclant declares from his cot.

They cannot turn a blind eye to whatever may be happing to these pitiable kids. Aside from that, they are going to need more provisions to make it to the top of the Parthectra Mountains. It is decided to rest up for a couple of days so that they can regain their own strength. Lonar, Slagradislaun and Larsynth have recovered with the most ease and they will do surveillance of the place to get a better idea of what the story might be.

Lonar and Slagradislaun head to the top of the hill the next afternoon. After a full day's rest with some food in their stomachs they are beginning to come back to normal already.

"My last attempt to make it over the hill felt downright impossible." Lonar marvels.

"I'm sure it did. Lifting my arm felt downright impossible yesterday." Slagradislaun understands.

They sit on the safe side of the mound's peak peering over. They watch for any sign of activity in the strange mini village below.

"It looks like nobody's home." Lonar says.

"Yep, not a soul in sight. Did Neras actually *see* anyone? Could his mind have been playing tricks on him?" Slagradislaun questions.

"We were all in pretty bad shape but he's adamant about those kids being chained up." Lonar confirms.

They sit, staring down at the cabins, pond and farm plots. Both are contemplating how long their watch should continue before returning to camp.

"Someone must be here tending to that garden." Slagradislaun points out.

Lonar nods. The two continue their stakeout for another hour.

Lonar turns to Slagradislaun, "We should head back to camp...What?" He can see from Slagradislaun's face that something is happening. He turns back to witness the saddest and most disturbing sight of his life.

Three portly men come tromping out of the big cabin. They are so massive that they waddle back and forth as they each make their way to a different smaller hut. Opening the chained doors, they disappear inside. Each of them returns to the courtyard carrying a thick manacle with five young boys attached to it and to one other by the ankles. The groups then move to one of the fields and begin to toil away. Once the men have emptied the five smaller cabins on the right side of the pond they move over to the left side cabins. This time the scene is the same, except with young girls. They make their way to the trees, harvesting the fruit.

Curiously, one of the small cottages on the left is not entered. Lonar and Slagradislaun spend the next few hours watching the men and the children. The hulking miscreants stand over the youths threatening them with a lash any time they slow or ask for a break.

"I can't watch this anymore." Slagradislaun growls.

"Agreed. Let's report back." Lonar answers.

"So, they're using them as slave labor? That's unacceptable! We must save them." Dervile jumps to his feet.

"I understand that this is a particularly sensitive subject for you, my friend," Eclant tries to calm him, "but we have to do this right if we're going to be of any help to them at all."

"Walk right into their cabin and stab them in their black hearts." Dervile demands, eyeing Slagradislaun.

Not sure how to react to that, Slagradislaun looks around to the others for help.

"Daddy!" Larsynth admonishes.

"Come now," Eclant reaches for Dervile.

"I don't see why that's such a bad idea." Neras puts in.

"I'm not sure what to think." Lonar admits. "It was a rather dreadful sight."

"We can't flippantly decide to murder three people in cold blood." Larsynth preaches.

"It isn't as if we don't like the look of them. These are terrible men, doing atrocious things." Neras retorts.

"There has to be another way." Larsynth pleads. "You can't ask Slag to do that."

No, of course not." Dervile recants, apologetically to Slagradislaun.

The next morning, Eclant promises to stay on the other side of the pond while the band executes their plan to free the enslaved children from the three monstrous men. From what he can see, everyone is in place. Neras is behind the main cabin next to the tool shed. Larsynth and Dervile are stationed in between two of the smaller huts on the left, containing the females. Slagradislaun and Lonar are both standing near the door of the hovel on the right, closest to the pond- farthest from the large cottage in the middle.

Although he is expecting it, Eclant cannot help but to jump a little at the sight of the flames bursting from the back shed. Neras makes his way behind the cabins to meet up with Larsynth and Dervile. The evil trio of men come rushing out of the cottage as speedily as their enormous girth will allow. They make a path for their burning building.

Slagradislaun goes to work picking the lock on the outside of the hovel. He is gratified to know that at least his people's chosen lifestyle is going to be used for good. He hopes he did an adequate enough job teaching Larsynth his technique. He is trying not to let his concerns for her cloud his mind as he needs to concentrate. The lock gives as he makes his last move. He pulls the chains off the handles, tossing them aside. Lonar steps forward kicking in the door to the cabin causing it to shake from the force. Slagradislaun disappears into the shack followed by Lonar. On the other side of the pond, a similar sight is being played out as Larsynth finishes with her lock.

She takes her first step into the tiny hut. The smell hits her like a wall, stopping her from moving forward. The awful conditions of the its inhabitants make her ill. Inside, are five teenaged girls, all of whom are chained to the walls by their ankles. They are filthy. She cannot discern what color hair any of them has from the thick layer of dirt that covers them. They each are dressed in what appears to be old seed sacks with arms and head holes cut in. None has anything to protect their blackened feet. The stench is overpowering. Larsynth blinks, trying to stop her eyes from watering. Around the room are three ratty cribs. Larsynth gasps at the sight. The five young girls startle at the sound of the door opening, each rushing to the nearest crib in protection. Larsynth takes a few slow steps forward, far enough to be able to see into the nearest crib, confirming her worst fear. Dervile's hand on her shoulder guides her to the first lock as he whispers,

"You have nothing to fear from us. We're going to get you out of here. But you all must remain quiet." He struggles to remain focused on the task at hand as he realizes that these girls are not far his own precious daughter's age.

No one answers as they look to one another for some sort of understanding. Larsynth unhinges the first lock and moves on to the next. Dervile is giving the girls instructions to take the babies and make their way around to the pond where Eclant is waiting. He will direct them to their camp on the other side of the hill.

Slagradislaun is moving through his locks with ease. Three of his five are already free

"You are safe. Go help as many of the girls as you can and wait for us with our friend on the other side of the pond. His name is Eclant." Lonar is telling them.

Unsure of the new strangers the boys remain in the shack unwilling to take the chance that this is a hoax and what awaits them outside is a beating by of one of their wicked captures. Not wanting to make them more fearful Lonar shakes his head approvingly,

"It is best if you all go together."

The fifth boy rubs his sore ankle. Slagradislaun turns to hurry out to the next cabin but finds Lonar and the four boys still standing at the doorway. Lonar is calmly trying to explain to them that everything is alright and they can leave but no one is convinced. Slagradislaun pushes his way by, stopping to say to Lonar,

"They can leave or stay but we have to move on."

Lonar understands and follows his friend out through the crowded doorway. While Slagradislaun heads to the next locking mechanism on the nearest hut, Lonar is gratified to see a couple of the boys timidly make their way out of the last cabin. Once the boys are certain they are safe, they spring over to the girls' hut where Larsynth and Dervile have been working.

"I think they're catching on." Lonar whispers.

As he hears this lock surrender to Slagradislaun he jumps to action kicking in the stubborn door. Five older boys jerk to attention at the clanking of the chains. Hoping the older group will be less fearful Lonar quickly explains,

"We're not here to hurt you. As my friend here gets through your lock, go across to the girls' cabins and help them around the pond to the old man. He'll take it from there."

"I'm not leaving." One of the boys declares.

Slagradislaun stops working the lock in his hands and turns to the boys. It is clear they are all in agreement.

Twenty-nine

"**A**RE YOU KIDDING ME? You want to stay here? Do you like being slaves?" Slagradislaun loses his cool thinking about what they are all risking to save these poor kids.

"Of course not!" The boy shouts back.

"This is our home. Our families have farmed this land for generations until those Doreg came and had their ghost kill our parents and they did this to us." Another boy explains.

"Ghost?" Lonar asks with alarm.

"That's what we call it, we don't know what it really is." The oldest boy steps forward trying to clarify, "It was invisible."

Lonar and Slagradislaun exchange a knowing glance. Lonar can see the anger building up in Slagradislaun's face before he turns back to focus on his second lock.

"I'm not going to creep out of my own family's home in the middle of the night." The first boy declares.

"Me either." The oldest agrees. He is now the third boy freed.

Lonar is not sure what to say to them. He can understand their drive to want to take back their own home but this was not part of the plan. It is too late to change it now.

"Look, I understand, let's get you all back to our base camp. We'll discuss coming and taking back your home after we get the girls to safety."

The boys all chuckle.

A cacophony of deafening screams rings out through the camp. Lonar jumps and runs to the door looking over to the other cabins.

Neras is stunned, he cannot believe what he is seeing. He is watching from the side of the largest cabin. He tries to keep his eye on the men battling his little blaze, and the hovels, to be sure everyone is making it out alright. He saw the younger boys come across to the first hut after Larsynth had it opened. The girls gave them three small piles of what looked like clothing. By now, they are half way around the pond heading toward Eclant. The girls have been waiting outside their cabin until the fifth one came out. They gather together in a huddle. Neras sees Dervile and Larsynth step out of the door making their way to the next cabin. The released girls start screeching and running, toward the fire.

"What are they doing? Are they going to put out the fire?" Neras fears.

Lonar and Slagradislaun are having the same concern as they come rushing out of the cabin they are in, chasing after the crazy girls. Neras hurries to the other side of the wall so he can see what is happening with this cracked gaggle of girls now, trying to determine when or if he should intervene. The men battling the blaze stop what they're doing. With each approaching step, the sound becomes clearer to them. They turn to see what is happening behind them. A new fire, the one in the eyes of the furious girls is more dangerous than the one they have been fighting. The men laugh preparing themselves to take down this ill-fated rebellion. They grab for the nearest rioter they can get their hands on. One man manages to catch two wriggling beasts. Two others banshees, though, run right passed him.

"Get them!" The oldest man calls as he has ahold of the hair of one and the arm of another.

A wild girl runs straight into the burning shed. The man chasing her lets out a snicker stopping his pursuit short of the heat from the flames. He turns back to the others,

"Well, that's one—"

Three metal points pierce his chest as the blood gurgles out of his mouth. The man slumps forward and slides down the prongs of the pitchfork. The oldest man screams out in anguish at the sight of his son's body. His grip loosens enough for the girls he has to break free. One of them jams her elbow into his throat, he chokes for air as he crumbles to the ground himself.

The girl who ran into the flames pulls the pitchfork out the back of the dead man. She sees the older man on the ground then reaches for something at the corner of the shed and tosses it to her sister who is standing over him. She looks in her hand and smiles back. She kneels down next to the man looking him directly in the eye, she lifts her arm high above her head before slamming down the point of a trowel into his windpipe. Seeing his father and brother meet their end the third man stops trying to grab for any of the girls and runs away from the camp as fast as his chubby legs will carry him. Lonar stops running toward the girls.

Across the pond Eclant is given the all clear signal. The young boys who had already made their way to him with the babies, assist him over to the middle of tiny village where Dervile, Larsynth, Lonar, Slagradislaun and Neras are gathering with the already freed children. The older boys are making their way over to them too as the girls relish their victory.

"Slag and I will keep working on the rest of the locks to get everyone else out of those awful shelters." Larsynth announces.

"Then, it's baths for everyone." Dervile adds.

"Thank you all for helping us. It won't be easy but I'm sure we'll be able to rebuild our lives." The oldest boy steps forward.

"We'll stay here for a couple of days to help." Neras says.

"Honestly, we could use more time to get ourselves to full strength after the long arduous trek through that accursed desert." Lonar adds.

"We'd be honored to have you all as our guests." One of the warrior women smiles.

"After everything is settled for you and we are refreshed, we can keep moving," Eclant steps forward, "Look."

He points in the direction behind the burning shed. "We're not far now. Do you think you'll all be okay without us?"

"He's never coming back." One of the girls looks in the direction of the still fleeing man as she wipes the blood of the other one on her sack.

"I guess you were right; we didn't need to get the girls to safety first." Lonar admits with a grin.

Thirty

"WE'RE MAKING GOOD TIME now that we're away from Zonthia." Dervile says, surveying the peak of the mountain.

Their trip has been progressing with more ease. This part of the elevation has fresh streams for water and is plentiful with game. There is a constant canopy from the trees offering them shade from the heat of the day as well as fuel for their evening fires. They have no trouble finding appropriate camping locations, often in a small mountainside cave. The only complaint that can be made is the length of the journey.

It has been three weeks since they fled the castle. Eclant has been healing nicely. He no longer slows their pace. Unwilling to accept his fate, he has repeatedly attempted to slide, but is not able. After the ordeal in the desert, they have become a more connected group. They spend few days in miserable silence as they did before. They expect to reach the summit in less than another week.

"I hope to never see sand again." Slagradislaun exclaims.

"Same goes for me," Neras adds. "I still haven't gotten it all out from between my scales. I hope we don't have any of the stuff in Narcor."

"I kind of liked it." Lonar jokes.

"That's good because you brought enough of it with you in your hair." Slagradislaun chuckles, pulling a bit of sand from Lonar's thick locks, flicking it at him.

"Yeah? You look jealous. Here, I'll share." Lonar starts rubbing his head on Slagradislaun. The two laugh and mock fight each other.

Larsynth rolls her eyes at their silliness.

"We need to prepare a camp before all the day's light is gone." Dervile does not want to sound scolding.

He enjoys watching them find happiness in spite of their circumstances. The lightness of their souls is refreshing in contrast to the direness of their quest and all that comes with it.

"My poor bow has been neglected. I'll go see what I can find for dinner." Larsynth offers.

"I'll go with you." Slagradislaun pipes up, skipping off behind her.

Neras and Lonar laugh together at Slagradislaun.

"He's not particularly smooth, is he?" Lonar grins.

Dervile flushes, pretending not to notice any of it.

Eclant shoots his friend a look. He is trying to read Dervile's thoughts on the matter but is unable.

"I'll go gather wood for our fire." Neras declare.

"I'll go with you." Lonar raises his tone in a sing-song mocking. He begins to skip with exaggerated steps. Neras lets out a roaring laugh that makes him exhale a flash of smoke from his nose. This only succeeds in making the two giggle even harder as they go off.

"I like to see them jubilant." Eclant says to Dervile. He is hoping to get a hint as to what the other is thinking.

"I also. I hope that it can last. This is a dangerous business we're up to." He says.

"It is indeed. I take it seriously and I believe that they do as well." Eclant reassures.

"I trust that they do. I fear that their youth shields them from the realities of what may come."

"I agree that it's likely the case. However, I wouldn't say I fear it. I would say that I pray it. I'm jealous of it." Eclant nods, sitting beside Dervile on the ground he had been clearing for camp.

"Indeed?" Dervile is incredulous.

"To be sure! Are you not?" Eclant is surprised.

"I suppose if I put my mind to it, I can see the virtue in it." Dervile allows.

Eclant is not convinced.

"If one may not see tomorrow, let him laugh today. I believe it." He looks to the sky.

"And if one may not see tomorrow, should he love today?" Dervile asks.

"Ah, you have noticed. Does it upset you?" Eclant inquires.

"As a father, of course, I want love for her but..."

"But this love would come with complications." Eclant shows his understanding.

"Under the best of conditions it would. These are far from that." Dervile shakes his head. "And this is sooner than I had expected to face such emotions. She is a child still."

"*Your* child she will always be. But *a* child? Not so, my dear friend." Eclant pats him on the knee.

"Are the fathers always the last to know?" Dervile sighs.

"Since the beginning of time, I trust." Eclant smiles.

Thirty-one

ATOP THE HIGHEST PEAK of the Parthectra Mountains the Oracle waits for the most unusual collection of residents of Dabrilas to ever find themselves working together.

He is an ancient being that has served Dabrilas since the beginning of its formation. He believes, that Death is too lazy to make the trip all the way up here to retrieve him. Regardless of if that's true or not, his life will continue on long after the world is turned to dust. He does not dwell on the perplexities of mortality. He has always been here and here he will always remain.

His body is fragile and he has no powers beyond the use of his OmniSight. His ashen skin hangs over his stone like eyes. It is difficult to determine when they are open and looking deep into you from when they are closed in silent concentration. Few hairs are left on his head but those that do continue to cling to his scalp are long and scraggly. Every movement is slow and deliberate. His speech is clear but soft and monotone. His character is indeterminable to all because he answers questions put to him and nothing more. Few alive today in the lower lands think him to be more than a bedtime story, though some yet believe. Only the most desperate and faithful attempt to reach him so far hidden in up in his fortress. Yet, for his part, he is aware of every life in the lands under his domain. An inquiry into any person's daily movements, deepest desires or future plans, he can answer. He knows each and every person better than any other living being. But, he is anonymous. He has no name. He thinks that he used to, but cannot recall what it is anymore. Now, he is The Oracle. It is a title, not a name but he is known as such.

Ducking his head as he enters the Oracle's dwelling Eclant is struck by how spacious it is. He hadn't imagined that at the top of the mountain, that has kept a watch over his long life of 428 cycles, there could be a wonder like this. His eyes take it all in. The entry is low for someone of his height. It is wide enough for the six of them to all enter side by side. The flicker of the flames bounces off of rock, providing an orange glow that lights every small recess of the mountainside cavern. In contrast to the spacious entry, the back of the cave comes to a point as the sides and top slope back to the spot where sits the Oracle. Eclant has heard tales of him since he was a small boy. For as long as Eclant has been in the world, he knows this man has been here far longer. Dervile, who himself has seen 867 cycles is but a youngster to this timeless creature.

The Oracle is perched on an unassuming throne cut out of the rock in the side of the cave. He motions to them to enter. They inch forward in awe. The Oracle looks at Eclant. The two consider each other before the Oracle points to the ground in front of him. Eclant continues on, more out of reverence than fear. He gives a bow to the wise man before crossing his long legs and lowering himself down; ignoring the little pain that still remains since his sliding had gone so awfully, painfully wrong.

"Ask me." Are the only words that are spoken by the Oracle to Eclant once he has taken his seat.

He has some understanding of how the Oracle is said to work, he will answer any question put to him. You can ask as many as you like, because no information will be offered beyond what you request.

"Is this a Time Lock?" Eclant begins, though he is certain that it is.

"Yes." Is his reply. Eclant thinks, realizing he may need to ask more specific questions.

"Is this a working Time Lock?" He clarifies.

"It is."

"Why was it put on me?" Eclant asks, to himself as much as to the Oracle. He does not really expect an answer.

"King Cryptis is trying to stop you from taking the Gem of C'Vard."

Everyone is startled at the reply. It is not that they do not expect that to be the answer. They did not think that the Oracle would have such information. Again Eclant pauses. Grasping how much the Oracle does know, he considers that he may be able to gain more information than he has previously thought.

"Can I ask you more than yes or no questions?" Eclant tilts his head to the side in confusion.

"Yes," the Oracle answers, not trying to be funny.

"Are Smaldi and the King working together?"

"Not anymore." The Oracle looks at Slagradislaun.

"Of course, yes." Eclant closes his eyes and shakes his head. The image of Smaldi's throat being sliced from behind flashes in his mind.

"How did Smaldi get involved? Did the King hire him?" Eclant fears.

"No, Smaldi has been following you. He overheard your plans. He then offered the information to the King."

"What does he hope to get out if it?" Lonar interjects.

"The opportunity to Time Lock you." The Oracle does not take his eyes off of Eclant.

He considers this. He cannot figure out how or why Smaldi could have managed to have jumped on him so quickly.

"Did Slagradislaun kill the future Smaldi, who was in a slide at the time?" Dervile speculates.

"Yes."

"That explains how he knew exactly when we would be there" Slagradislaun adds.

"It also means that Eclant is going to do something significant enough to Smaldi in the future that it will make him go to such lengths to prevent him from being able to slide." Dervile works out.

"That information has died with Smaldi and as far as he is concerned I do not have time to worry about it now anyway." Eclant dismisses.

"How *exactly* does a Time Lock work?" Slagradislaun asks, trying to get as much useful information on the thing as they can.

"Once applied to the neck of a Darist, a Time Lock, blocks that Darist from sliding to any other point in time or from ever sliding back to the time that it is being worn, if it is ever removed."

Eclant jerks at the second part of the explanation. This he has never heard before.

"You mean if I get this thing off tomorrow, for the rest of my life, I'll never be able to slide into today or any time since this accursed thing was put around my neck?"

"Correct."

"How do we get it off of him?" Neras asks.

"The key to unlock the device is a hair from the head of the one who put it on you. It must be inserted into the lock from the highest point of the Darist homeland under the SightMoon.

"When is the next SightMoon?

"735 days from now."

"We don't have that kind of time." Larsynth shrieks with alarm.

"We have no choice, dear." Her father pats her hand trying to hide his concern.

"Is there any other way?" Eclant pleads.

"There is none."

"What are we going to do?" Lonar asks.

"We're going to have to go after the Gem without my ability." Eclant tries to sound strong for everyone's benefit, including his own.

"The King knows what we're trying to do. That's going to make things impossible." Lonar points out.

Neras drops his shoulders, fearing his people will be stuck here forever, destined to die off. Lonar shifts his weight in determined energy to take on the King. Larsynth squeezes her dad's hand who squeezes back. Slagradislaun and Eclant are overcome by thoughts of the day they were ambushed in the castle and how they could have stopped it. The Oracle wonders if they will have any more questions.

Thirty-two

"**I** THINK WE NEED TO FIND OUT as much as we can about the Gem of C'Vard from the Oracle." Dervile tells everyone after they have a chance to absorb what they were told about Eclant and the Time Lock.

"Does the King have the Gem of C'Vard?" Lonar asks.

"Yes." Is all the Oracle says in reply.

"Is it at the castle?" Lonar continues.

"Yes." Is again all that the Oracle mutters in the affirmative.

"Is he using it to control the people of his kingdom?" Larsynth pipes in.

"Yes."

This is not getting them as far as they have hoped.

"I believe that we need to slow down and think about how we ask these questions so we are not still at the top of this blasted mountain at the next Sight Moon." Eclant interrupts.

"You're certainly right." Dervile agrees, then pauses to formulate his next inquiry.

"Tell us everything we need to know about the Gem of C'Vard." He quizzes the Oracle who, himself, tries to hide a grin of appreciation for such a shrewd probe.

"The Gem of C'Vard has a long history, but pertaining to your quest specifically, this is what you need to know." The Oracle begins. "The dragons of Narcor have been the guardians of the most precious and dangerous items of Dabrilas. Items that are not safe to take the risk of them falling into the wrong hands. A little more than two centuries ago, the Gragin clans arrived in their new homeland given to them by the King of Zulbarg for whom they had assisted in a recent siege against his kingdom by the neighboring King of Jalib. Without the Gragin, Zulbarg would have fallen and the King exiled."

Lonar nods at the pieces of the story he does know.

"Within the decade, that King was murdered by his brother who took over the throne. He was never comfortable with the Gragin being given land so near to the kingdom. It was his fear that it is too dangerous as the Gragin were expert warriors who could conqueror his territory. However, the people of his kingdom have long memories and would forever think of the Gragin as their saviors. They wanted the Gragin there, looking over them, as they often said. He tried many things but could not sway his people to rid the kingdom of the heroic Gragin."

"This is where the deception begins." Lonar conjectures.

The Oracle nods.

"Thus, he came up with a plan. He had heard stories of a Gem black as midnight that can be used to instill fear into hearts of whoever he chose. It is known that it was be kept in Narcor with the dragons. So, the King went to his dungeons and picked his three most prolific thieves. He offered freedom and a pardon for life to whoever could retrieve the Gem from the far away world. It took another decade, but one of his thieves returned to him with the mysterious Gem in exchange for his pardon. What he found though is the tip of a sword for all of his trouble."

By now everyone is sitting around the Oracle on the ground of the cave, children enthralled in the story.

"The King then sent his envoy to the dragons to tell them that the Gem had been spotted and it is believed to have been stolen by a nefarious band of warriors that refuses to leave his land. He claimed they robbed, attacked and pillaged his kingdom. As it was their sacred duty to all of the inhabitants of Dabrilas to keep dangerous objects like the Gem safe, they sent a large group of their most diligent and fearsome dragons to retrieve it."

The Oracle looks up to study the faces of his audience avoiding the penetrating eyes of Eclant. This is the most talking he has ever done. He was asked to give all the information which pertained to them and that is what he is going to do.

"I think we know what happened from there." Lonar stops him, looking to Neras for confirmation.

"Yes, thank you. So, where precisely is the King keeping the Gem now?" Neras asks, careful with his phrasing.

"It is hidden in the seat of his throne under the cushion."

"Well, how's that for security?" Dervile chuckles. "So, it obviously does not need to be in physical contact with a person for it to work on them. Am I correct?"

"That is right."

"That's a relief." Slagradislaun admits.

"How can it be destroyed?" Neras inquires.

"The best way to combat fear is through truth. Hold it and speak a most honest and deep truth." The Oracle answers.

"Let me get this straight. We have to break back into the castle, sneak our way to the throne room, hoping that the King is not sitting on his perch. Then, we remove the royal cushion and find the Gem. Next, we hold it and tell it our deepest darkest secret?" Neras is incredulous.

"The truth you must speak may be more difficult than you realize." The Oracle corrects.

Eclant nods, understanding what the man means.

"Often, the most truthful thing you can say, is something you haven't yet managed to admit to yourself. I believe that what will be required to destroy something as devious as the Gem of C'Vard is a special and profound honesty. You may be surprised by how hard that part of our mission will be." Dervile tries to explain to the younger ones.

He doubts that they are as of yet capable of grasping what he is attempting to get through to them.

"It's late. We must sleep." Eclant declares in a daze.

There is something about the Oracle that bothers him. He cannot figure out for certain what it is. Perhaps, he is tired from the difficult journey or the stress of the news he has heard about the Time Lock. He thanks the Oracle for his assistance and precision.

He tells the rest of the group to use this time to consider any more specifics they may need or anything clarified by the Oracle in the morning.

The Oracle knows there will be no further questions which will be unfortunate for the band. He sneers knowing they will return, weakened and he can do what he must to stop them then.

Thirty-three

THE FOLLOWING MORNING the group says their farewells to the Oracle.

"Could you tell us of a way to return to Zulbarg that will bypass the desert of Zonthia?" Dervile inquires.

The Oracle confirms that there is and draws a map in the dirt for them.

"Why didn't we come up that way?" Larsynth questions.

"It is a way down not up." The Oracle grins.

Eclant bows his head and thanks him for his hospitality previous evening. He is still preoccupied by some odd sense about the man. There is something about his eyes, but Eclant can't put his finger on it.

They walk the whole first day in silence. Everyone spends the time reflecting on what they have learned. Eclant, most of all, is engrossed in his own thoughts. He is not surprised to confirm that he is, in fact, caught in a Time Lock or that Smaldi is working with the King, for whatever reason. In all of the stories he has been told about Time Locks from the older generation, never was it explained that not only can one not slide while ensnared but that he will not be able to slide back to this time period, ever. He had not expected to hear anything of the sort from the Oracle. He is distraught by this additional restriction. Besides that, he is going to have to manage to get his hands on a lock of his enemy's hair which will undoubtedly be more difficult now that he is dead. However, he had no expectation that the removal of the object would be dependent on a specific date, particularly one so far away.

Dervile's thoughts mostly turn to his friend, Eclant. He aches for what pain Eclant must be going through. A Darist that cannot slide. After all that Eclant has done in the past to help keep him, his family and many friends safe when they were being hunted; he knows he cannot let Eclant go through this on his own. Once this business with the Gem is settled, he will request Eclant's further assistance in helping Slagradislaun rid his people of OverSight. Then, the two of them will, together, do whatever it takes to remove the Time Lock and release Eclant from this portable prison.

Slagradislaun considers what they have learned from the Oracle. He fears that killing Smaldi could have been a terrible mistake but, at the time, he believed that it was the only way to get Eclant free. Under these new circumstance he believes it may be best to put his plans on hold, at least until they recover the hair from Smaldi. Once that is accomplished, there will be nothing more they can do for Eclant until the next SightMoon. He figures, that since there will likely still be a great deal of time to spare; they can still rid the world of the curse that his people bring to it due to their OverSight. Either way, he knows he will remain in Eclant's service until the end of his ordeal. It is the least he can do.

Lonar tries to keep his mind on the task at hand but, he cannot help it wandering. This is the first time he has allowed himself to really think about the loss of his brothers, his family, everyone he has ever known and his home. He is more alone walking with these other five people beside him than he ever has been before. As much as he wants to destroy the Gem and free the people of Zulbarg from their King; he does not know what will be next for him. There is a real possibility that he may not make it through the upcoming events. When he lets himself dwell on that thought he is not able to work out how he feels about that outcome.

Neras cannot shake a pestering idea of how they will manage to break into the castle again in order to get near to the Gem. He is not able to see how the raid can be a success. First, they have to get passed the gate, then through the town, into the castle and all the way to the throne room without causing alarm. In a place where fear and suspicion reign supreme. He considers every possible subterfuge but nothing will work. Except one dangerous option but he knows it is their best chance.

Larsynth is keeping her eyes on the others. Their faces are showing that they are all preoccupied deep inside themselves. Her heart goes out to Eclant. She does not think she could get over the loss of her ability. It is so much a part of who she is. She knows it has to be a terrible injury to his soul. She notices that her dad keeps watching his friend with flashes of pity and empathy crossing his face. There is no doubt that they are going to do anything that is necessary to remove that wretched thing from his neck. The other three, which she now considers "her boys" are unusually quiet. A tender comradery has developed between them on the long, trying journey up the mountain. They often tell each other stories, hunt, play games and tease each other. Now though, each has his own thoughts to wrestle with instead of one another.

Thirty-four

A WEEK HAS GONE BY since they left the Oracle in the direction that he told them about, hoping for a shorter return trip. Also, one that does not require the treacherous passage through Zonthia. The group is getting restless as they have yet to confirm that this is indeed any faster than backtracking would have been. Leading the others, Slagradislaun stops.

"I think I know what the Oracle meant when he said this was a way down and not up." He points to the end of the trail.

The others gather around him looking out over the side of the mountain.

"Is this what he meant?" Lonar is suspicious.

"Well, it is a short cut that's for sure." Dervile tries to calm everyone else.

"I think I can glide down from this high up but I doubt the landing will be pretty." Neras offers, trying to ignore the pained look on Lonar's face at the recollection of his two previous failed attempts at flying.

"I'm going to guess we're a little over 75 feet above the water up here. As long as it's deep enough we should be fine." Slagradislaun offers.

Everyone looks around unsure what to think or say. Are they really going to jump?

"Let me go down first and test to see how deep it is." Neras insists stepping forward to the edge.

"Are you sure you want to do that?" Lonar touches his shoulder, proud of him.

"It makes the most sense really." Eclant agrees.

Turning back to the others, Neras attempts a confident smile before making a running leap into the air. As soon as his feet leave the ground, his wings pop open. They are small and weak but the wind catches them all the same making his descent a slow one. As he approaches the water he flinches, fearing it may be too shallow. His body plops down into the liquid. He looks around making sure he is safe. He realizes that nothing hurts. Neras screams with glee as he bobs around in the deep water, not finding the bottom.

"Come on down. It's nice." He calls back up to the others.

Not needing to be told twice, Slagradislaun takes three steps back before running off the edge of the mountain. He closes his eyes. He splashes down much harder than Neras did but he breaks the surface of the water unscathed. One by one the others follow. They all take some time to splash around in the refreshing pool.

"This sure beats the Zonthia desert." Lonar says floating on his back.

"That probably took a week off of our journey." Looking back up the mountain Dervile calculates.

"We'll be back to Zulbarg before we know it." Eclant smiles at the shortened travel time.

But this realization is sobering for the group. They begin to think about what is to come, cutting their joyful reprieve short. They all begin to make their way to the shore on the other side of the pool to continue on their somber mission. Neras is the first to reach the coast and pull himself out of the cool water with a little help from Lonar and Slagradislaun pushing him from behind.

Their assistance is a bit more forceful than necessary causing him to teeter right over on to his belly. The pair lose themselves in laughter at their friend's predicament, which they caused.

"Come on now boys, help him up."

Eclant tries to hide his chuckling at the sight of the dragon's feet flailing about in the air. He reaches down to assist Dervile out of the water, who is also laughing at the image. After hopping out of the pond themselves, Lonar and Slagradislaun each grab one of the dragon's claws and walk him back into the upright position. He brushes himself off with a grin. Getting free of the water Dervile turns to help his daughter maneuver the hard to manage footing of the wet sand. She is nowhere to be found.

"Lars!" He screams in alarm.

Everyone else recognizes the sound of terror in his voice as he continues to cry out for her. They are all begin calling her name and searching the area.

"Wait, wait, look!" Eclant shrieks pointing to a faint ripple coming out from the center of the pool with a few bubbles now breaking through the water.

"She is still in there, under the water!" Eclant concludes.

Lonar jumps in followed closely by Slagradislaun. They both push themselves under the water but it is too murky to make out what anything is. They resurface, treading water as they search around with their arms, frantic to find any hint of where she may be. Lonar spies something over near where the side of the mountain meets the pool moving about. He rushes over to it.

"She's over here!" He calls out to Slagradislaun who comes barreling over faster than a fish.

He dives down finding her arms floating lifelessly. He tries to pull her back up to the surface but she caught on something. Lonar now too is doing his best to free her.

"Something has her leg." He shouts to Slagradislaun.

He propels himself back down under the water. He does not know how much time has passed now, but he knows she cannot stay below much longer. He is particularly concerned that she has stopped struggling. Slagradislaun grabs her leg following it to her ankle where he feels something thick and slimy trying to pull on Larsynth. He shoots back up to Lonar.

"Keep a hold of her! It's trying to tug her under!"

Lonar reaches out getting a hold of her wrists doing his best to yank her back up. He refuses to let go or be defeated in this potentially fatal game of tug-of-war. Slagradislaun takes a deep gulp of air preparing for his next descent. Reaching the mysterious foe once again, he seizes it with both hands desperate to free Larsynth. No matter what he tries, he cannot loosen its grip on her. Something cold rubs against his arm. His hands grab at it, fearing he is next. Relief over takes him as he comprehends what it is, a dirk. The one from Larsynth's boot has floated out and is now tightly clutched by Slagradislaun.

He takes a couple of well-placed swipes trying to cut Larsynth free. The blade slices the side of the monster releasing part of her leg. He knows he is making progress. Again, he strikes out at the creature, this time with more force and speed. He becomes furious with rage. He attacks it over and over until pieces of the massacred beast begin to float up to the water's surface. He struggles to regain control over himself. Doing so, he returns to Lonar who is now carrying Larsynth out of the water and over to the others. Reaching the shore, he sets her down where Dervile and Eclant take over her care. Working on draining the water from her lungs and trying to rouse her back.

Slagradislaun reaches the others in time to hear her cough. Eclant rolls her on her side to get the rest of the fluid out. Dervile rubs her back as he struggles to fight the tears betraying his false portrayal of calm. Slagradislaun drops to the ground beside her exhausted from the rescue. As she looks around to everyone grateful for what they have done. She reaches for Slagradislaun who pulls her toward him with both of his arms. She sees her dirk in his hand. She looks in his face seeing the fatigue and emotion. She puts her palm out; he places the weapon in it. She replaces it in her boot then rests her head on his shoulder.

The journey the rest of the way back down the mountain is less grueling than it was going up to the Oracle. By this time, the wounds that Eclant has endured as a result of his multiple slides have healed completely. Traveling downhill as opposed to uphill the group is able to make it to the base of the mountain two weeks faster than it had taken to reach the top. As they walk and camp each night there are many discussions about the best way to get the Gem away from the King. Neras has come up with what, all agree, may be their best chance. At first, they are opposed to Neras placing himself so directly in danger but after days of no better options they eventually come around; except for Larsynth. The only other hope is that since they have been gone for more than a month, the King might believe that they have given up.

"It's hard to decide which is stronger with that man, his fearfulness or his arrogance." Lonar ponders.

"Let's hope for our sakes it's his arrogance." Dervile adds.

Thirty-five

B Y THE TIME THEY ARE OUTSIDE the Ashford
forest, the six have what they believe is a solid plan
for gaining access to the castle. It all hinges on Neras.
The other five each take their positions around the outside of the
city wall not in sight of the guards. They will soon know if their
friend has been successful on his quest. If not, he is surely dead.
They all try to put that possibility out of their minds even though
it is real. If there is no sign of Neras' return by sundown then they
will meet back together at the spot in the Ashford forest where
they had made camp the last time they attempted to gain access to
the Gem, but failed.

Lonar looks at the shadows all around him trying to figure
out what time it may be and how long has Neras been split off
from the group. It was barely daybreak when he left. Lonar
estimates that it is about midday. He makes his way to
Slagradislaun who is bedded down not far from him.

"He's probably about reaching them now." Lonar declares.

"That's what I was guessing too." Slagradislaun confirms
looking off in the direction Neras has gone. "Do you think this
will work?"

Lonar takes a long time to answer.

"I really don't know what to think. I hope so."

"Me too." Slagradislaun chuckles at the absurdity of the need
to say so.

Lonar tags his arm playfully and smiles. It is nice to have relief from the severe gravity of what is actually happening.

"I can't stop thinking that we've sent him to his doom." Dervile jumps at the sound of his daughter's voice.

"What are you doing over here?" He scolds her. "Get back to your position."

"We're not ready yet. I've got plenty of time." Larsynth cannot take one more minute of sitting there alone, convinced that she will never see Neras again.

"He's confident that this will work. We have to trust him."

Dervile places his arm around her shoulder and pulls her in close to him. Larsynth closes her eyes and pretends she is still a small child and there is nothing bad in the world. She wants to call the whole thing off and sit right there with her dad protecting her, forever, if possible.

"It probably will be any time now." Dervile works out for himself.

He smiles at her, thinking how perfectly she has turned out. His hand reaches out and touches her cheek, caressing it. Larsynth leans into his touch until he is supporting her head with one hand. She twists her hips, lowering herself to the ground and places her head on his lap. He smiles down at her, mentally invoking every powerful being he can remember from every tale he had ever heard begging them all to keep his little girl safe. He does not believe in any of the fairy tale gods but, just in case even one of them is real he is determined to have his prayer heard.

Eclant looks around to the others. Lonar catches his eye. The two motion to each other that it is about time to give up hope. The sun will be coming down soon. Lonar sneaks back over to Slagradislaun. Tapping him on the arm he says,

"I think we might as well head back to the camp site." Slagradislaun looks up to the sky seeing how dark it is getting. He nods in agreement. They both look to Eclant who bows his head to indicate that he understands what the conversation they are having means.

Larsynth has been sleeping on her dad's lap for hours and is disoriented when she opens her eyes. She sees the bottom of her father's chin as his face is lifted up to the sky. It is dark. She knows what that means. Neras has failed. He is gone. She cannot contain her grief at the realization. She rolls over, burying her face in the lap she has been sleeping in and sobs. Dervile pats her looking to the other three. Seeing Larsynth fall apart like that makes the reality of the situation hit each of them in turn. Neras is certainly dead.

Grief replaces the anticipation of battle that the five of them were thriving on all day. One by one, they bow their heads in reverence for their fallen comrade. They do not know what is going to become of them next. They still have an important mission that they believe in and so did Neras. Lonar knows in his heart that he cannot let this go, the King will pay and the people will be freed. He also will avenge Neras' death, he promises himself that above all, he will make them pay.

Slagradislaun and Lonar stand up and begin walking toward the Ashford forest so they can all discuss what will be their new plan. Looking at Eclant, Lonar cannot figure out what he is doing. He appears to be pondering the sunset. His head is tilted to the right and he is squinting. He begins to swing his arms. He cannot shout out or they will all be discovered. He jumps about doing his best to get everyone's attention. Lonar is watching Eclant trying to decipher what the meaning is behind his odd behavior when Slagradislaun smacks his back and points at the skyline.

Dervile and Larsynth stand up and turn around to see what the other three are watching and pointing to. The sight is amazing. At first, it looks like a flock of birds, but as they get closer the clearer it is that these are larger than birds. Twelve large dragons are flying out of the horizon as if they were given birth to by the sun itself. They are heading straight to the town. Lonar never thought he could find a sight like this anything but blood chilling but in this moment it is beautiful.

Thirty-six

THE PEOPLE OF THE TOWN are screaming and running in all directions. The terror of the image of the dragons flying at the kingdom has taken hold of everyone. It would have done the same even if the people of Zulbarg were not predisposed to being abnormally fearful. As the horde comes closer to the walled fortress, the townsfolk decide that it is time for them to get out. The first pass over the kingdom, all twelve let lose the most devastating blaze they can muster. Rooftops are burning all over the city causing more hysteria. Before long, the throng is beating on the gates demanding to get out so that they can escape into the nearby forest. Their heightened level of fear leads to all out panic which eliminates anyone's ability to think clearly. Unfortunately, due to the frenzy the manic inhabitants trample their fellow citizens. The scene is shear pandemonium. Children are left standing in the streets crying and terrified while their parents are swept away in the chaos. As the first wave of deserters make their way out of the city limits the smoke becomes thick enough to choke those remaining.

The dragons make multiple passes, being certain that every thatched roof is ablaze. Once their job is complete, they perch themselves on the top of the stone castle. They want to be there to witness that what they have been told by Neras is not a lie. They need to see the Gem of C'Vard for themselves. They have little care whether or not it is destroyed. The guardians of the piece believe that it is their duty to see that they are fully aware of whatever will happen to it next. They do not want to take a chance that this is all a rouse of some sort. The story Neras told them went against everything they have believed about the Gem and the reason why they are stuck so far from their home. Like they have done to the Gragin and their village, they will destroy everyone in this place, burn it to the ground and tear it apart until the Gem is found and they are able to return home and save their offspring. They are not going anywhere until this has been seen through to the end.

The five partners gather together away from the burning town.

"This isn't how it's supposed to go!" Lonar has to scream above the crowd to be heard by the others. "I knew we shouldn't have trusted those devils. They'll destroy everything!"

"These poor people!" Dervile agonizes at their plight and the hand he has in it.

Slagradislaun points to the sky again. This time the view is harder to make out. It looks like the thickest dragon they have ever seen. As it approaches, they can see why. It is two dragons. One flying while the other one rides on its back.

"Neras!" Larsynth is overcome with joy at the sight of him.

The group is confident that the dragons showing up means that their friend is safe but there is nothing like seeing him for themselves to confirm that he is. The wind and dust pick up as the large dragon lands next to the group still standing outside the wall of the city. With his hind legs firmly on the ground he stands straight up as Neras comes tumbling down his back. Without so much as a glance to his passenger, he is up and gone to perch on the castle with the others.

Neras looks around in disbelief. The destruction is incomprehensible to him.

"Did my people do all of this?" He asks, though he is sure that he already knows the answer.

"Yes." Slagradislaun shouts. "What did you tell them to do? Burn it to the ground?"

Neras bore the unfair accusation in stride.

"I told them to fly over a couple of times to scare the people and create a bit of panic. I never said anything about setting fires." He assures everyone.

They readily believe him. The horror on his face is enough to convince them that this is not something he would have wanted.

"What do we do?" Larsynth asks looking from person to person for an answer but finding none.

"I don't think there is much we can do at this point." Her father says.

"This is our fault. We're supposed to be helping these people and now they have lost their homes and everything they own. I'm sure some have lost their lives in there!" Larsynth cannot stand the thought of all the suffering.

"I don't disagree with your concerns, but this is our chance. The guards have all abandoned their posts and are trying in vain to stop the fires. We have to go now!" Eclant stomps one foot on the ground.

Lonar looks into each face to see if he can judge what they are thinking. He knows Eclant is not wrong. Now, is the time. What is more, he cannot let this all be in vain. If these people are going to suffer through losing everything they own he is going to make certain that when they return to rebuild their lives at least they will do so freely and without the influence of their King. Lifting his broad sword high above his head he lets out a blood curdling scream and runs forward into the smoke and flames. He is going to end this, all of it, the Gem's control over these innocent people, the King's reign, the dragons, everything. The fury rises up from deep in his soul. His new friends see in him this pain and know that it is in control of him. They cannot let him face this alone. As Lonar is engulfed in the smoke he disappears from view. All five of his companions run off after him. They are in this together.

Thirty-seven

THE TOWN IS EERILY EMPTY of its people. Fires blaze on from every direction but the streets are clear of the usual congestion. The smoke stings their eyes as they try to take in the devastating scene. A shiver goes down the spines of the onlookers as they are unprepared for what they are witnessing. There are bodies strewn on the ground like discarded trash, trampled in a stampede of frightened chattel. Mongrel dogs graze without fear of reprimand on the bread and fruits that are now dotting the walkway around the village as the food carts had been overturned in the rush to escape. Fabrics and goods are tossed about in the muck like worthless trinkets; all that was once for sale is now without value.

"I can't believe what I'm seeing." Neras glares at the top of the castle to the dragons that came at his bequest.

"They were supposed to scare them. This..." the words are choking him.

"Is not your fault." Larsynth finishes his sentence. "You couldn't have known they would do this."

She comforts him reaching for his shoulder but he turns away from her.

Lonar is fighting himself from speaking up. He has dealt with the dragons all of his life and while they are not to blame for the Gem and the misinformation they were given; he knows all too well of their brutality. This is no surprise to him, but that fact is not doing anything to suppress his outrage.

Eclant and Dervile continue to stand in silent awe.

"We must go." Eclant manages to pull his stare away from the horrendous sight.

Most of the King's guard are attempting to save as many of the buildings from the flames as they can. This leaves the route to the castle wide open for the band to make their way with ease. The six turn away from the disturbing view before them to continue on their duty. Lonar keeps his eyes on where the guards are at all times, he does not want to take any chances of being stopped now that they are so close. Relief overtakes the group as they file into the castle entryway. Believing that they are safe from danger, they smile at each other and prepare for the final leg of their long undertaking.

Lonar has been in the castle twice before but he has never seen the throne room. As far as castles go, this is not a large one. The entire kingdom itself is not more than one hundred acres.

"This long hallway leads to a stairway that will take you up to the King's private rooms." Lonar reports the little he does know about the castle's layout.

"Usually the throne room would be easily accessible from the entrance. Most people who ever enter a castle go to the throne room it is the only public part of a Royal's dwelling." Eclant points out.

"True, and the public won't be walked passed the King's quarters so the throne room must be down here before the stairway." Dervile surmises.

They all begin heading down the long hallway looking in every side room they come across, as Slagradislaun had done the last time they were here.

Slagradislaun stops in the passage. He lifts his hand pointing ahead. The rest of the group looks in the direction of his gaze. There it is. There is no doubt. Outside in the hall, they can tell from the oversized entrance that this is the threshold to a large room, one unlike any of the others they have passed so far in their search. When they had been here before the entrance was covered by floor to ceiling crimson velvet drapes. The immense drapery is now pulled aside, framing the entrance to the room that they had previously veiled. Slagradislaun never got the chance to check that area as they had been ambushed in a room not as far down the hall.

They huddle up together making their plans.

"Slagradislaun, since you're the fastest and will still be invisible, you go in first and head straight for the throne. Find the Gem quickly." Eclant tells him.

"The rest of us will be right behind you in case there are any guards or townspeople who decided to take cover in here. Let's try to not cause any more suffering to those who are innocent in this mess." Dervile looks around to each one of them for confirmation. Their faces answering for them.

"I want the King." Lonar makes it clear to everyone. "I want to be the one to make sure that he cannot hurt anyone else. I need to be the one that stops him from manipulating these people. I know the stories, but I believe that my people are partially to blame for all of this. If we hadn't helped the kingdom fight off the Jalib stronghold, none of this will have happened to the Gragin, the dragons or the people of Zulbarg."

"There would be no people of Zulbarg if your clan hadn't helped them. Besides we cannot start going around on every little detail that lead us to this place. We're here now, so let's get the Gem and destroy it." Slagradislaun knows this train of thought can lead to a back and forth between Lonar and Neras that he is in no mood to sit through right now.

"That poor excuse for a King is hiding from all of the chaos outside. He's probably in his chamber under his bed like a terrified child." Neras says with a gleam in his eye at the mental image it brought to his mind.

Thirty-eight

SLAGRADISLAUN ENTERS THE HUGE STONE ROOM, the sight in front of him stops him in his tracks. He is about to turn back to prevent his friends from coming in after him but it is too late. They all cross the threshold. The band pauses to take in the spectacle. There he is, sitting on his throne holding court with imaginary subjects, is the King. All of the death and destruction of his kingdom is of no concern to him as he is perched on his regal seat without a care in the world. The six are gobsmacked at the crassness of his actions.

"I must admit; I was beginning to think you all had given up on your silly little quest. You want revenge?" He sneers, looking at Lonar.

"This is about more than that." He barks back.

"Hand over the Gem." Neras demands.

The King panics as he sees he is greatly outnumbered. Reaching his hand down the front of his robes he pulls out a whistle. He raises his hand to his mouth and takes a deep breath. Lonar lunges forward, trying to stop him from raising the alarm but he is too late. The room fills with guards. Two move in on either side of the King, as three line each of the two walls and three more come in behind them from the entrance, trapping the group in the room.

Back to back, the comrades know they will have to fight. Lonar and Larsynth face the King and his guards. Neras has his back to them facing the entrance and the three guards that have come in behind them. Dervile and Eclant are facing the three guards on the right of the throne with Larsynth at her father's elbow. Slagradislaun is opposite of the two old friends facing his own threesome. Everyone readies their weapons.

Slagradislaun pulls his daggers out and positions himself for a fight. He knows he will have one chance to strike before he is seen. He makes his way out and around the three he has been facing, making each footfall soft and soundless. As far as they are concerned, no one is preparing to take them on as each of the intruders is facing some other direction. The room is still. No one wants to make the first attack. Slagradislaun knows this is the time to make his move. With a dagger in each hand he pulls his arms back until his elbows are nearly touching behind him. He releases, jabbing one dagger into the back of each of the two guards in front of him. The third bouncer hears the gurgle of blood in the victims' throats. Slagradislaun pulls the daggers from their targets. Twisting his waist, his arms follow the momentum allowing the sharp blades to slit his throat. The last of the three guards' bodies drops to the floor.

The other sentinels see that the attack has begun. The room is a blur of activity as each aggressor takes on his opponent. Lonar's rage has the chance to release itself and it does. He explodes forward toward the guard across from him. Slicing at him. The sentry drops his weapon and grabs at his stomach. His hands reach down to cradle his intestines as they fall out. Lonar is so out of his mind that it does not register that the man is dead. His corpse falls to the ground but Lonar continues to stab at it before he stops and looks around to see how his friends are faring.

Neras swats away the three men's swords as they take turns halfheartedly trying to pierce the monster's thick scales. None of them has ever seen a dragon in person let alone try to fight one standing directly in front of them. Neras trusts that, for now, he is in no danger. The look of him is enough to keep his foes off their abilities. The King sees this pathetic display put on by his men and is infuriated.

"Stop messing around and kill the beast already!" He screams.

Neras knows he has no choice. One of the men lifts his sword over his shoulder preparing to take a big swing at his neck. He does not want to, but it is him or them. Neras lets out burst of fire shaking his head back and forth sure to engulf them all, not watching. Their charred remains fall at his feet. He cannot stand to look.

Eclant swings his rod from the head of one opponent to the other, smacking them so hard that they cannot manage to get their baring in between beatings. One of the men crumbles to the floor unable to control his legs as the sense has been knocked out of him. Eclant uses this opportunity to lift his staff above his head to deliver a final blow to the other. He feels the skull give way as he brings it crashing down.

Dervile is left fighting one on one with the third guard that confronted him and Eclant; he is struggling through the battle. The man has him at a disadvantage. With death all around him, Dervile is gagging at the strong rancid stench that accompanies his ability as a NecroSight. He manages to thwack away the man's sword with his staff a few times but he keeps coming at him. He is being forced backward. Dervile stumbles to the floor with his foe over him about to strike. Larsynth sees this out of the corner of her eye. She, too, is fighting the overpowering distraction of so much death. The room is filled with smoke acting out scenes making it hard to remain focused. Fearing for her father, Larsynth turns away from the enemy she is fighting to plunge her dirk into the back of her father's attacker. Her man sees this chance.

Thirty-nine

WITH HER ATTENTION TURNED AWAY from the guard, Larsynth sees that her father is safe. She sighs in relief. Her head turns back to her enemy to see his blade coming toward her face. She manages to pull herself back away only to have it swipe across her right cheek, cutting it. She screams out in pain grabbing for the wound. She is disoriented as the warm blood flows through her fingers and down her chin. The attacker again lifts his sword to come back at her. As he opens up his body to take the final swing, two daggers appear, sticking out from his neck and chest.

Larsynth looks up to Slagradislaun with thanks for the help. Lonar rushes over to the King who is now left vulnerable as they have finished off all of his guardsmen. He pushes the tip of his broad sword into the King's throat.

"Get up." He demands.

The King raises his hands in a show of surrender but does not move. Dervile races over to his daughter. He rips a part of his shirt and presses it firmly to her bleeding check. Slagradislaun walks over and removes his daggers from the dead man. Instead of replacing them in their sheaths he holds them ready in his hands, watching the King.

"I said, 'Get up.'" Lonar repeats with more force and hatred in his voice.

Eclant turns to the scene.

"We know all about the Gem and we know where it is." He says looking at the throne.

Larsynth's pain is eased as she looks into her father's eyes. He smiles at her, both of them are relieved that the worst of their task is over.

The look on her father's face has changed. He no longer is smiling. Blood begins to trickle out from his lips.

"Dad!?" She screams.

He is not responding. His hands let go of her and reach toward his chest clasping something. Larsynth looks down to see the point of a spear breaking forward from his torso. She lifts her eyes back up to his. Dervile drops to the stone floor.

"NO! DAD!" Larsynth shrieks.

Neras turns their direction to see that the man Eclant had beaten with his staff is now standing over Dervile's body. With one quick swipe, he knocks the man away from Larsynth and her dying father. The guard slams into the wall, before he can regain his balance the dragon takes a deep breath and sets him ablaze. This time, there is no remorse.

Larsynth kneels next to her father. She places her arms around his shoulders and pulls him in close to her chest. Larsynth closes her eyes and pretends she is still a small child and there is nothing bad in the world. She wants to call the whole thing off and sit right there with her dad protecting him, forever, if possible. Her hand reaches out and touches his cheek, caressing it. Dervile leans into her touch until she is supporting his head with one hand. She twists her hips, lowering herself to the ground and places his head on her lap. She smiles down at him mentally invoking every powerful being she can remember from every tale she has ever heard, begging them all to keep her father safe. She does not believe in any of the fairy tale gods but just in case even one of them is real, she is determined to have her prayer heard.

Eclant is next to them with his hands on the chest of his old friend trying in vain to stop the bleeding. He knows it is not going to work but he cannot bring himself to give up. Tears are streaming down his face as he pleads with the old man not to leave him.

Dervile looks his daughter in the face making sure she is looking back into his eyes.

"Look here Smidgen, you have to fulfil the promise I made to that young man." His eyes look over to Slagradislaun. "There is so much about it that you don't know. You'll have to have help." Dervile searches around the room but he cannot see Neras or Lonar. "It will mean great sacrifice on your part but it is time. It has to be done. Now, promise me."

Larsynth is not interested in helping anyone else do anything. As far as she is concerned the end of the world is happening right here and right now. Nothing else matters. She cannot find a way to respond to his request. She stares at him trying to take in every inch of his face so that she never forgets it. Her insides are being torn out of her and there is nothing she can do to stop it. Her soul is screaming out in torment but her mouth cannot make a sound. The thickness of her anguish weighs her down until she does not think she can ever move again.

"Promise me." Dervile struggles to reach his right hand up to his face kissing it.

Larsynth can see how important this must be to him. She grasps his hand and places it on her heart. She lowers her chin to kiss her palm. Before she can get her lips to it, it is filled with her tears. She kisses the saltiness and places it over his ever slowing heart. Dervile looks to Slagradislaun again, then to Eclant and finally to his precious girl. It looks like he wants to say something but nothing comes out. His head falls to the side as he breathes his last.

Eclant lifts Dervile off of the floor with a strength he has not had for some many years now. Larsynth sits staring at the pool of blood on the stone. She hears rustling coming from behind her. It is the King. Her inner sorrow numbs her mind. She has become two persons inhabiting the same space. She raises up from the floor. Before anyone can comprehend what she is doing, she seizes Lonar's wrist and pushes the tip of his blade into the King's throat. She leers at the dying man with satisfaction as the blood runs down his purple robes, staining them like he has stained everything.

Forty

NO ONE MOVES as the King's body slumps over the arm of his throne. They are all in shock at what they have witnessed. Dervile is gone. It is not real to any of them yet. Eclant stands in the middle of the room cradling his dead friend's body like a baby.

"Lonar, get the Gem!" Eclant yells out to him.

Larsynth walks over to Eclant and places her hand on her father.

"I'm sorry, sweet girl." Eclant softens his voice. "But we must complete the Gem's destruction or this would have been for nothing" He explains to her.

"Yes, of course, that's what he wants. Wanted." She corrects herself running her fingers through his long hair as blood from the wound on her check drips onto his snow-white locks.

She stares at her father but sees nothing. Her eyes go in and out of focus, as does her mind. She turns around and stomps back to the throne. With no regard, she grabs the King by the arm and tosses his body aside. Her four friends look to each other with wonder and fear. No one wants to get in her way. They leave her alone. She looks around seeing the shock on their faces.

"Well, this is where the stupid thing is, right?" She shouts to them.

Larsynth then turns back to the throne and begins ripping at it trying to get the cushion off or pull it apart. She is having no success. Again, she looks around at the stunned faces.

"Is anyone going to help me here or have you all turned to stone!?"

They jump to action. Lonar and Slagradislaun run over to the chair and help her tear the cushion off. With a few strong punches of Lonar's fist, they break through the wood on the top of the seat. Larsynth reaches her hand into the dark void searching around. She stops moving. Her face registers that she found something. She pulls her elbow back away from the chair and tugs her arm a few times until her hand comes free. She turns back to the center of the room. She raises her hand in front of her chest, showing everyone her treasure. It is a perfectly round ball of the deepest black.

"So, I have to say something truthful and it will be destroyed?" She asks Eclant.

"It will seem so." He answers. "At least that's what the Oracle says."

"I don't regret killing the King!" She screams at the Gem.

With baited breath they all are watching the Gem expecting it to burst into a million pieces.

Nothing.

"That's the truth." Larsynth argues. "I really don't."

"Well, maybe on some level deep down..." Slagradislaun starts, knowing better than anyone how taking a life leaves a mark on your soul.

"I don't!" She insists throwing the Gem as hard as she can on the stone floor.

It bounces then rolls over to Slagradislaun's feet. He picks it up to try.

"I killed my family." He admits, but the Gem still does not react.

"I have the feeling that we are not thinking about this right. The Oracle says we have to speak a deep truth. I believe what he meant is that we have to make a confession. Something you have never told any other living soul and haven't admitted to yourself."

No one moves. They are contemplating what Eclant has said and are trying to come up with anything they can think of to confess. Lonar considers for a long time before he drops his sword. He walks over to Slagradislaun and puts out his hand. Slagradislaun sets the Gem in his palm. Lonar closes his fingers around it keeping it secure. He then turns and walks over to Neras.

"Together?" He asks, looking Neras in the eyes.

He shakes his head and reaches out his large claw. Lonar opens his hand so that Neras can place his on top of the Gem.

"I never cared at all about saving the people of Zulbarg from their awful King or this stupid Gem." Lonar admits.

The Gem shakes in their hands. One small crack appears along the side.

"I also didn't care about getting the dragons back to their home because of what is happening to them. I want them gone because I don't like or trust them." He divulges looking at Neras, ashamed. "I wanted revenge for the deaths of my family."

The Gem cracks more.

Neras knows it is his turn to have his say. He opens his mouth but nothing comes out.

Slagradislaun looks at him with sympathy. He knows how hard this is for him. He walks over and puts his hand on Neras' shoulder, reassuring him.

"It's okay." He whispers. Neras looks to him with a tear in his eye before turning back to the Gem.

"I don't care about my people or what is best for them. I don't care about going back to Narcor except," He pauses trying to admit to himself first. "I want to be like the other dragons. I hate being so small. I hate that I cannot fly. I'm not a real dragon. I want to be a real dragon. I don't care about any of the rest of it. Who cares if someone stole a stupid Gem? Who cares about the dragon name and our dishonor? I'm sick of not fitting in anywhere. I don't belong with them because I'm too small and I don't belong with you because I'm too big..." As Neras continues on, the Gem is breaking apart in their hands.

Neras does not realize that it is working.

"Lonar is the first friend I've ever had and because my people are so awful and single-minded he will always hate me because of who I am and what *other* dragons have done. And there's nothing I can do about any of it. I feel so alone, it hurts." Neras bursts into tears.

With that confession, the Gem bursts out of their hands. A million tiny pieces slip through their fingers and are raining down into the blood that covers the stone floor.

Forty-one

THE GROUP LEAVES THE CASTLE to show the dragons the remains of the Gem in hopes that they will return to the mountains as agreed. Even though without them, their plan could have never worked, they are still upset with the useless destruction they brought down on the town and the people. Neras watches them fly away back toward the caves. His confession is still weighing on him. He had not realized until he spoke the words how bitter his feelings towards his own people are. He is sad and ashamed of himself.

Slagradislaun and Lonar are heading into the forest in hopes of finding the fleeing citizens of the charred city. As they leave the stone wall walking toward the woods they stop. The forest is coming to life. Between each of the trees are people walking toward them, hundreds of them coming out of the darkness back to the city. They are not fearful, instead, they are resolute. They will bring their homes back to life. It will be difficult to rebuild but without the curse of the Gem on them, the people will be able to reach out and ask for help from other kingdoms around Dabrilas.

Eclant finds an empty cart with straw and gently lays his friend down into it. Larsynth stays by his side holding his hand. She will never be the same. Though he is the one who died, she too will no longer live. She is not sure if she can go on without him. She has no desire to bother trying.

Lonar and Slagradislaun return to the town as the people do not need their convincing. Neras and Eclant meet them by the gate.

"Now what?" Slagradislaun asks, looking around to the others.

"I think I need to spend some time with my own people." Neras glances toward his mountain home.

"That's a fine idea." Eclant pats him on the back.

"I want to find some appreciation for who they are and try to help make them better. We have a long road ahead of us still. We have to get back to Narcor. Destroying the Gem of C'Vard is the first step for us."

"I plan to be there to help you for the next step." Lonar grasps the dragon's claw in his own hand. "I am and will always be your friend. I was the first and I intend to stick around until the end." He smiles. "In the meantime, I think I will stay here and do what I can to help the people rebuild. I am akin to them in a strange way. I'm hoping this will also help me to become more familiar with the rest of Dabrilas. I've been shut up in that village all of my life. There's so much more out here to see."

"These people are lucky to have your help. I am as lucky, if not more, to have your friendship." Neras grins at him.

"I will take my old friend to his home land so that he can make his journey to the sky as he should." Eclant nods to the cart where Larsynth is sitting holding on to her father. They all bow their heads in sadness.

"I would like to go with you two." Slagradislaun admits.

"I know she made a promise to her father, but I'm afraid son, I don't know if you can count on her fulfilling it." Eclant warns.

"I'm not thinking about that right now." Slagradislaun defends. "I have no other place to go and I want to help Dervile. I owe him for all he was willing to do for me; a stranger, who he never treated like one."

"I understand." Eclant relaxes his voice. "I think having another young person around will be good for the girl anyway."

"Don't forget." Lonar looks around to everyone. "We have a date. The next SightMoon we're taking a trip." He nods.

"Of course." Neras agrees.

"Won't miss it." Slagradislaun adds

"Oh, you don't all have too..." Eclant begins.

"We're doing it together." Lonar insists with the two others agreeing. "While you're gone I will do what I can here to find that devil's hair for you."

"I'm touched and taken aback by you all. Thank you." Eclant says earnestly, fighting his tears.

They all stand there in silence, each privately recapping everything they have gone through together and wondering what is still to come. They look over to Larsynth sitting in her grief, wishing there was something more they could have done to protect Dervile. Each will mourn him in their own way.

Eclant tugs on Slagradislaun's arm and the two take their leave. He pats Larsynth on the head and climbs into the front of the wagon, taking up the reigns. Slagradislaun decides it is best to leave her to her silent suffering for now and joins Eclant in the front. The horses begin to trot out of the gates and off to Dervile's homeland.

Neras and Lonar give each other one last look. They both know that neither of them would be here without the other. There is a bond here that cannot be broken. Without a word, Neras turns, walking through the gate he continues up through the path back to his home and his people. Lonar watches him for as long as he can still see his tail swaying behind him. He knows it will not be long until they are together again.

Forty-two

"**I** KNOW WHY YOU'VE COME, dragon." The Oracle declares without turning around to face the beast standing in the entryway to his cave.

"They succeeded in destroying the Gem." The voice booms behind him.

"Yes, I'm aware. It's no consequence." The Oracle reassures.

"It is to me. I need the Gem of C'Vard for the other dragons."

"It isn't the only way."

"Are you sure?"

The Oracle laughs.

"This is no laughing matter. I am old. I need assurances my quest will not fail after I'm gone."

"Have you come to me for a reading or do you expect me to make those assurances to you?" The Oracle grows angry.

"I've come to make sure you're going to be good to your word." The intruder sneers.

"And I will."

"I need to hear you say the words."

"I will not let you down." The Oracle confirms.

"Look at me and say it!"

The Oracle turns to look upon his guest, glaring into the hollow space that once was occupied by his right eye, "As I have told you in the past, Veralke, neither you nor any other dragon of Dabrilas ever set foot on Narcor again."

"Excellent."

Made in the USA
Charleston, SC
15 May 2016